Joseph Bayma

The love of religious perfection

Or, How to awaken, increase, and preserve it in the religious soul

Joseph Bayma

The love of religious perfection
Or, How to awaken, increase, and preserve it in the religious soul

ISBN/EAN: 9783741190032

Manufactured in Europe, USA, Canada, Australia, Japa

Cover: Foto ©Andreas Hilbeck / pixelio.de

Manufactured and distributed by brebook publishing software
(www.brebook.com)

Joseph Bayma

The love of religious perfection

No one can read, in the proper Spirit, this valuable Treatise, without perceiving it well deserves the reputation it has won. Learning, wisdom and piety, unite to recommend it to all who wish to advance in that best and purest of all Sciences, the Science of Salvation. Like two other similar works, the Imitation of Christ, and the Spiritual Combat which have helped to enlighten and encourage thousands on their way to our only true home, you may open this little book at almost any chapter, and find something to turn your thoughts heavenward; to raise your heart to God, to purify its affections, to warn you against the deceitfulness of Sin, and the allurements of the world in the midst of which we live, and must, nevertheless, by all means, work out our Salvation. "Be ye perfect, even as your heavenly Father is perfect," said our divine Redeemer to the multitudes who followed Him. And of these, where was the greater number to live and die, but in the midst of the same cares, distractions, temptations, dangers that fill up our every day life? The general state of society was moreover very much the same for them as it is now for us; agitated by wars and rumors of war, by great political changes, and by nearly every kind of public calamities.

To all therefore, and all times such works as this are highly useful; and to such as will profit by the experience and wisdom they teach, better by far, than treasures of gold, and precious stones and the purest silver.

The translation now offered to the public was made in England, and imitates successfully the simplicity and unaffected style of the original, whose merits are so great, that it was almost universally attributed to the pen of the Very Rev. Father Rhootaan, late General of the Society of Jesus: an error which it was found necessary to contradict in the Bibliothèque des Ecrivains, S. J.

Since 1851, when this treatise first appeared in Rome, it has passed through many editions in different places, and has been translated into several languages. May the perusal of it here increase in many souls the love of solid virtue and perfection which it is so well calculated to inspire.

BALTIMORE, *January*, 1865.

I HERE present you, religious reader, with three little books on the pursuit of religious perfection, which, though small in size, are however for that very reason most adapted for constant use. My design in writing them was not to render service to others, but to excite myself by the best means in my power to carry out in practice the full idea of religious life. And this is why, after having selected and portioned out in articles the chapters on each subject, and arranged them in order, I cared but little for other ornaments of composition; and looking to the matter rather than to the words, my only desire was to present in plain and simple, not to say, careless diction, the words that most faithfully portrayed the idea which I had formed in my mind. Nor can I say that I saw any reason for endeavouring to aim at a more elegant style when I begun to think of publishing them; for though there may be some whose approbation is more easily secured for the matter itself by presenting it in an elegant and polished form, I know that most people, in their desire to promote their perfection, either do not pay much attention to examining the gracefulness of the language, or if they do meet with anything of this character, are distracted in their thoughts and prevented from receiving more ample fruit. For it is a peculiarity of the human mind to seize and turn more readily to account what is said in an ingenuous, and so to speak, simple manner. Of this we have many

instances in other books, but I know of none more
striking or more beautiful than that of the Holy
Scriptures and the Imitation of Christ, whose style I
was led to follow closely by my own inclination and
an unceasing perusal of it.

With regard to the subject matter of this work,
being of opinion that the entire study of perfection
might be embraced under three principal heads, viz:
the motives, means, and exercise of virtues, I thought
that I could not do better than divide this little
treatise into three books, each one of which should
correspond to one of the aforesaid parts. It is true
that I have touched on only a few of the many subjects that readily presented themselves to me, but
they are, I think, of the most solid character, and
faithfully collected from the opinions and precepts of
antiquity. And hence, however much those other
ornaments of style, by which the minds of men are
wont to be captivated, may prove wanting, I still trust
that the soul which is really enamoured of virtue will
find matter herein wherewith to arouse and strengthen
itself more and more.

It is then with perfect confidence that I beg to offer
to you, with a few suitable additions, what I have
from time to time experienced to be of such great
assistance to myself, in order that, even amid such an
abundance of the very best books, you may be able to
make a diligent use of this poor aid of mine, to advance the pursuit of religious perfection.

ROME, *June 29th*, 1851.

CONTENTS.

BOOK I.

THE

LOVE OF RELIGIOUS PERFECTION.

BOOK I.

THE MOTIVES WHICH SHOULD URGE THE RELIGIOUS TO PROCURE THE PERFECTION OF HIS STATE.

CHAPTER I.

Of Vocation to Religious Life.

1. *The Spirit breatheth where He will,* and calls and entices men to the love of holiness divers ways.

One is raised to high contemplation, another is marked out for a life of action, and external labour, and both by the Holy Spirit.

Some, uniting action to contemplation, not only study to present themselves holy before God, but aid their neighbour unto salvation; and this is the most perfect and most divine of all.

Still one and the same is the Spirit which guides all, and which by such divers ways conducts all to the same end.

2. Let each one walk with care and solicitude in the way, in which the Spirit hath called him, if he will please God, and arrive at the perfection proper to him.

For if he neglect or despise the care of his own perfection, truly it will be a marvel, if he ever gain life eternal and the happiness promised to the faithful followers of Christ.

He, that followeth not the path marked out for him by the Spirit, shall seek with great peril for another one to gratify his self-will.

3. Many are called by the way of tribulations and persecutions, and great will be their error, if they seek for peace before the time.

Many are called by the way of poverty and humility, and woe to them, if they desire to live at ease, and be held in esteem.

Others are invited by the way of silence and solitude, who will not be saved if they remain in the world.   ·

Thus one is called this way, and another that; but all by the same Spirit, which is to be obeyed and followed by all.

4. Think not thou hast done anything great for God, because thou hast followed the good Spirit in choosing so perfect a state; for it is rather thou that hast received a great favour from God, in His having called thee and chosen thee.

For many were called with thee, but few were chosen with thee; it is then a great favour, that God has not only called thee like the rest, but chosen thee for so holy a profession.

It is a great favour, that He has freed thee from all care of worldly things, that thou mayest attend to thyself in perfect leisure.

It is a great favour, that He has left

temporal and earthly goods to others, and kept Himself and the treasures of Heaven for thee.

5. But thou art not yet in safety, nor canst thou ever be certain of thy salvation, lest thou become proud or careless in the service of God.

And if thou do not by a love of perfection prepare thyself with all diligence against temptation, thou canst not hope with reason to persevere in thy vocation.

Labour the more, saith St. Peter, *that by good works you may make sure your calling and election.*

And the Prophet also saith: *Such as turn aside into bonds, the Lord shall lead out with the workers of iniquity.*

But if any one strive not to advance day by day by good works, his vocation and election are most uncertain and on the verge of ruin.

CHAPTER II.

That Virtues are to be sought for with Constancy and Diligence.

1. WE must not think that the time will ever come, when we may lawfully desist from the pursuit of perfection, or become slothful and remiss therein.

Virtues are barely acquired after much labour, and are quickly lost by idleness.

Thou art not yet perfect, be thy progress what it may, for it is written: *He that is just, let him be justified still;* and, *Be you perfect even as your Heavenly Father is perfect.*

Something always remains to be pruned away, even after a life of a hundred years and more, spent in religion.

For we are ever mortal men and liable to evil affections, which, though they may be cut off and kept down, cannot be wholly rooted out.

2. We know not the dispositions of God in our regard, and what may befall us, in punishment of our negligence and inconstancy.

2*

We know not whether He may not have decreed, that on our progress should depend the salvation of many men, whose blood He will hereafter demand at our hands.

We know not that violent temptations are not about to come upon us, which will require greater perfection in us, if we would overcome them.

3. So then we must not set to our holiness any limits, beyond which we will not pass.

They, that fear not to set a limit to their holiness, slight the call of God, and throw themselves into the greatest danger.

As God called many other Saints, whom we honour in His Church, so also has He called us.

And therefore as they hearkened to His call and never paused in their pursuit of virtue, so let us also walk worthily in our vocation with great hope, and serve God with gladness.

4. No one is more disposed to make

rapid progress, than he that humbly makes
an entire offering of himself to God, and
presumes not to refuse Him anything whatsoever.

For nothing is more pleasing to God,
than this humble confidence and greatness
of heart.

O how quickly should we learn all perfection, did we offer ourselves thus generously to God!

How quickly should we become Saints,
if, with great promptitude and good will,
we said to God with St. Paul: *Lord, what
wilt Thou have me to do?*

5. But this is the work of a soul free
from evil desires, and of a heart enamoured of humility.

Wherefore we must, above all, fight
against the corrupt inclinations of our
heart, and cleanse our soul from all evil
habits, that we may prepare an abode for
the Lord.

Then, saith the Lord, I will come to that
man, and I will make My abode with him
and dwell with him for ever.

CHAPTER III.

That the Multitude of our Defects should urge us on
to procure our Perfection.

1. EXAMINE thyself and consider attentively how many faults thou hast committed, how many thou still committest,
how few good actions thou hast performed,
and how imperfectly even those few.

What hast thou hitherto sought after
with so much care and fatigue? in whose
service hast thou spent thy labour, thy
strength, and thy time? Is it in Mine and
that of thy soul, or rather in the service of
vanity and sensuality?

Behold thy time draweth nigh; then
thou shalt open thine eyes, and to thy
great sorrow find nothing good in thy
hands, wherewith to enter into the kingdom of Heaven; but thou shalt find many
sins for which thou shalt have to satisfy in
fiery torment.

2. It is now many years since thou wast
bound to seek thy perfection; hast thou

lived perfectly even one month or one
· day?

Thou shouldst be daily most intimately
united to Me by heavenly contemplation;
and behold thou hast not as yet consecrated
entirely to Me one single hour without
defect.

What hast thou done for Me? what hast
thou suffered for Me? what great or heroic
action hast thou hitherto performed for My
sake?

For it will be thy only comfort in death
to have satisfied, by the practice of penance
and other virtues, for thy defects and sins.

8. Consider, moreover, how unwillingly,
and impatiently thou bearest contempt,
how easily thou breakest forth into complaints, and fillest everything with thy
lamentations and murmurings!

How vain and unmortified thou art, since
thou dost so ardently desire to be honoured,
and seekest by thy humiliation to be exalted and promoted, even in the school of
humility!

How slow thou art to wear hair-cloth!
how sensual at meals! how inordinate in
thy drink! how delicate in sleep! how attentive to thy dress! how desirous of a
comfortable abode! how opposed to everything that is repugnant to the love of the
flesh!

How lavish and immoderate in vanities,
how slothful and tepid in virtues!

How captious and hard to deal with!
how haughty and indiscreet in thy replies!
how obstinate and refractory in obedience!

How ill-advised and disorderly in loving!
how inconstant and distracted in praying!
how slow and reluctant in keeping silence!
how imprudent and arrogant in speaking,
how inconsiderate and worldly in writing,
how vain and licentious in thinking, how
irreligious and scandalous in acting, how
puffed up and empty in discoursing!

O how often art thou angry and inclined
to grow hot against thy brethren! how
seldom dost thou give them an example of
patience and humility!

How often art thou overcome by sloth! how seldom dost thou rouse thyself to prayer and meditation!

How often dost thou complain of thy superiors or equals! how seldom dost thou look to thy own defects and imperfections, in order that thou, too, mayest amend thyself!

How often dost thou omit good through human fear and respect! how seldom dost thou abstain from evil actions for love of Me!

How many sins, either known or hidden, thy own or of others, that thou hast not yet expiated at all! how many dost thou daily add to be expiated in a future world!

Why then dost thou delay or hesitate? It is thy own affair, it is thyself it concerns; and, therefore, thou must needs labour diligently and manfully.

Thou shouldst also strive to advance every day, even a little, by a good demeanour of life, if thou love thyself, and desire to arrive at My glory.

CHAPTER IV.

That the Consideration of Purgatory conduces to the
Amendment of one's Life.

1. SON, how long, thinkest thou, wilt thou be detained in the pains of Purgatory?

For few only, who have had a great desire of mortification and purity of heart, have deserved to escape those pains.

If thou wouldst endeavour to imitate them, thou mightest then hope not to suffer long in those flames, but to be soon carried into holy light and glory.

But if thou overcome not the flesh, and strive not against ambition, thou wilt be long and painfully tortured.

2. Purge away thy sins now whilst there is time, and deny thy evil desires, for so it will be better for thee.

For now thou wilt purge them away, both with less pain, and with a great return of merits.

But he that waits to be purged and sifted by that fire will suffer far greater and more horrible torments, and will acquire no merits from such suffering, because time shall be no more.

3. Or dost thou think that the things that thou reservest to be purified in that terrible fire are but few, or of no account?

Deceive not thyself: *I will search Jerusalem with lamps, and I will judge justices; and in My sight no man living shall be justified.*

What often appears to thee excellent and worthy of reward, is an abomination before Me, and to be atoned for by punishment.

For nothing defiled or soiled shall enter the holy city; for the place is holy, and the resort of all purity.

4. Better then is it for thee to do penance now with merit, than impose a new burden of sins upon thee; for thou hast far too much to correct and amend.

If thou wilt endeavour to pay off now

3

2. *Blessed are they that hunger and thirst after justice, for they shall have their fill.*

O that thou wouldst hunger and thirst after justice, that thou mightest at length understand the truth of My promise, and being filled with delight, not turn aside to the consolations of the world.

For whence are the wars and contentions in thy heart? are they not from thy concupiscences that war in thy members? Fight therefore against thy concupiscences, and thou shalt attain victory and peace.

3. It is in vain to seek for peace from any other than from Me; for the heart is not filled by earthly joys, but is weighed down and afflicted the more, as soon as they have passed away.

Moreover I fill human consolations with bitterness, that thy soul may have no repose in them.

And I daily permit many trials and tribulations, that they who stay far from Me, may more speedily return to me with joy.

But if any one come to me with confidence bearing his cross, and despising all things for Me, he it is that knows how vain and fickle is all worldly consolation, and he rejoiceth more in detesting his sins and in a victory over himself, than the whole world in its useless and false joys.

4. Wherefore make a beginning, son, fear not; overcome thy concupiscences, spurn thy ease, and take away all vanities.

Give thy mind to prayer and compunction, read the lives of the saints, meditate on thy last end, be solicitous to cleanse thy heart, and thou shalt find peace.

Be humble and sober, and thou shalt find peace.

Be courageous and constant, and thou shalt find peace.

Be patient and diligent, and thou shalt find peace.

If in this manner thou bearest My yoke and My burden, thou shalt receive a hundred fold in joy, and possess life everlasting.

3*

Chapter VI.

That the fear of Hell should increase our Love of Virtue.

1. *He that thinketh himself to stand, let him take heed, lest he fall.* For many have fallen away from the way of salvation, because they would not take heed of the danger of falling.

Had they thought of the pains of hell more frequently, perhaps they would not have fallen, or would have quickly risen.

Be not deceived; though thou hast many motives for hope, still thou shouldst not long forget those, that strike a holy terror into the heart; neither a holy vocation, nor the religious habit, nor the dignity of the priesthood rendereth thee secure. Not a few have begun well and ended ill, because they presumed that they had already a certainty of their salvation.

2. Think, I beseech thee, what a miserable thing it is to be stripped of all good, through one's own fault, and racked with

every torment amid the devils! To have tasted a short pleasure against the will of God, and then to dwell in eternal fires! To have sought an idle gratification on earth, and to have found through it most bitter wailing in hell!

Think over the tortures of the martyrs, how many, how varied, how horrible! Behold they are nothing, if compared with the torments of hell.

The martyrs were sustained by the greatness of the reward at hand, by an ardent love for Christ, by the purity and security of a good conscience, by the grace of God that sweetens every pain, and by a most holy cause for suffering; but nothing of all this can be imagined in hell. ·

3. There the torments give not merit, nor purify, but they inflict vengeance.

There no love soothes their suffering, but hatred and despair sharpen it the more; no grace consoles or refreshes, but the Almighty vengeance of God strikes dismay into them with its scourges, and makes them more sensible to pain; no peace of conscience, but *the storm of darkness is reserved for ever.*

O how hard it is to be without God, to be in a pool of fire and sulphur, to be tormented by the devil, in the company of all the wicked!

How bitter to remember the past, to look at the present, to think of the future! The momentary pleasure of the sin has passed away, but its punishment shall never pass away.

How serious will those things then appear, which used to appear to the sinner of little importance, but were the beginning of his damnation.

4. O my religious brother, think not that these things apply only to seculars; thou too art a man; *take pity on thy own soul.*

Though thou mayest have wrought miracles, *be not high minded, but fear;* for the higher the place whence thou fallest, the more dangerously art thou wounded.

They that are nourished delicately during life, are the first to putrefy when dead. So they that are nourished in a peculiar manner with heavenly food, and fall away from the spiritual life, more quickly fall into the depth, and contemn their danger; so that the saying is very true, *the best when corrupted becomes the worst.*

What cures others, is of scarce any service to them; what moves others, has lost by long habit all efficacy with them.

5. O how sincerely should we humble ourselves, we that can yet fall and perish for ever!

With what solicitude should we cleanse away our past sins, lest perchance, when weighed in the balance, we be found wanting.

How piously should we obey divine inspirations, and make our life conformable to our profession, lest we deserve to have our portion with hypocrites!

CHAPTER VII.

That it is dangerous to desist from the Pursuit of
Perfection.

1. BEWARE, son, lest thou begin to turn
aside from the way of perfection, and it be
not well with thee.

Thou hast abandoned all vain and worldly things for My sake; already a great reward is prepared for thee, and it shall not
be long deferred. See that thou now turn
not back again to thy utter ruin, to those
things which thou hast so generously despised.

Let not the labour of advancing frighten
thee; behold, however great it may be, it
cannot last long.

This life glideth on, and *the figure of this
world passeth away*, and when thou thinkest
not, the day of reward will dawn.

If thou walk with constancy in the way,
which thou hast entered upon, for My sake,
fear not; thy sorrow shall be turned into

joy, and thy joy no man shall take from thee.

But if thou begin to desist, although what thou neglectest appeareth of little account, still thou immediately growest weaker, and more inclined to fall.

2. Be not deceived; if to-day thou begin to grow tepid in thy prayer, and give way to voluntary distractions, to-morrow thou wilt be still more tepid and distracted in mind.

If to-day thou curb not thy senses by mortification, to-morrow thou wilt find greater difficulty in girding thyself for the struggle.

If to day thou allow thyself to be seized on by vain and useless things, to-morrow thou wilt cling ·still more closely to them, or be fixed in even worse.

This is the just penalty inflicted by Me on those, that shun the labour of fighting, who, because they have the grace of gaining the victory, but neglect it, deserve to be stripped of this inestimable grace.

3. We must never desist from the fight, until, having overthrown all our enemies, we receive the crown of victory.

The devil has deceived many by a foolish security, whom he had attacked for whole years in vain by other temptations.

For the spirit is subdued by the negligence that springs from such security, the habit of heavenly thoughts is lost, the more powerful protection of the Divine mercy is driven away, the love of an injurious liberty is nourished, concupiscence is roused, the strength of the soul is weakened, the rebellion of the senses is increased, sins are daily multiplied, and the way is paved to• perdition.

For the senses of a man are inclined to evil from his youth, and therefore, if the curb be removed, they will rise in rebellion, to his grievous destruction.

Behold I have said to thee: *If any one will come after Me, let him deny himself:* and, *The kingdom of Heaven suffereth violence, and the violent bear it away.* For unless thou fight against thy vices and overthrow them, they will vanquish thee, and subject thee to the slavery of the devil.

4. Whoever takes no care to advance, hath already begun to retreat, and become worse than he thinketh.

If thou wilt preserve what thou hast, aim at what is more perfect.

For the weakness and imbecility of the human will is very great, and it will be no small thing, whilst thou strivest to ascend to higher sanctity, to persevere in thy present state.

Nothing stands still in this transitory life, but we see that all things are changed in their turns. God alone, with whom there is no change, no shadow of vicissitude, remaineth the same for ever, and can never fail.

Now every man is like unto an evil field, that cannot be long without evil fruits, unless he be cultivated with all diligence by the exercise of virtues; and like unto a little bark, violently dragged down

4

the impetuous course of the stream, which cannot remain in the same place, unless it be impelled by sturdy strokes against the current.

5. Encourage then thyself, and whenever anything troublesome occurs, struggle even unto victory with a noble and constant mind.

Often it is not a great thing that troubleth thee, and draweth thee away from spiritual exercises; and if thou resolve to persevere, thou wilt often find the struggle to be shorter and easier than thou didst believe.

The struggle is shorter and easier to the watchful and diligent, than to the tepid and lover of liberty.

For he, that courageously resists from the beginning his sensuality and temptations, thwarts and deranges by his diligence all the arts of the devil; but he, that indulges his whim, and seeks vain distractions on every side, becomes weaker every day, and less capable of victory, and hence he is easily put to flight.

The enemy would not easily overcome thee, if thou wert at once to shake off thy torpor, and didst with a good purpose of fighting approach God in prayer.

Yea, the devil would even become weak, and would often fly in terror from thee, lest, perchance, thou shouldst obtain greater merit by reason of his temptation.

But if thou prefer to be torpid, and shrink from the fight through a mischievous idleness, or considering within thyself the good that thou hast already done, become little solicitous about the devil, thou wilt afterwards find to thy cost what strength and courage thou hast given him for thy own destruction.

CHAPTER VIII.

That it behooveth us to lay up Treasure in Heaven.

1. BE thou a good merchant whilst thou hast time, and prepare for thyself in Heaven a treasure that faileth not, *where no thief approacheth nor moth consumeth.*

What art thou doing? Behold thy years glide swiftly on, and death approacheth, and still thou showest no desire of solicitously making up the loss.

One day, one hour, one moment of time is able to bring in a return of very great merits to the man that diligently serves God.

Every good deed whatsoever, every thought, or good desire is recompensed with a great reward in the kingdom of Heaven.

Every victory over self, and even the slightest mortification and abnegation of the passions, cause us to be raised many degrees in the sight of God.

For what is at present momentary and light of our tribulation, worketh for us above measure exceedingly an eternal weight of glory.

2. Why then do we delay laying up for ourselves a great weight of eternal glory?

Why are we so ungenerous and sparing towards God?

Why do we weigh and consider so minutely, how far the mere force of obligation presses us, and neglect and almost despise, as though it were injurious, whatever does not seem to be obligatory?

3. Truly our evil desires blind us, so that we not only do not consult this our own greatest interest, but do not even fix our eyes upon so great a good.

Truly the children of this world are more prudent, far more prudent than we are, in their generation.

For they toil and labour for trifling riches, put themselves to great pain for a vain honour, suffer much and are prepared to suffer still more for a little power, and the brief happiness of an uncertain life,

4*

and do not even seem to feel the hardship of the labour; and still they are not certain of attaining to what they hope for.

But we, for riches that are above all price, for true and eternal glory, for the crown of justice, for happiness that surpasseth all conception, refuse to do these very same or less things, to suffer the very same or less pains.

And if at any time we have done or suffered something for God, and the salvation of our soul, although it be a mere nothing and scarcely sufficient to atone for our sins, forthwith we proceed with confidence, forthwith we reckon ourselves quite rich enough, and by our idleness miserably languish and become decrepit.

4. O dreadful blindness of men! where hast thou ever seen a merchant, that, having made a trifling sum of money, has rested from his labour, and said, I have enough?

How then is not he blind, who thinketh that he has sufficiently merited eternal glory, which as yet he possesseth not, and desists from laying up treasures?

Let us humble ourselves before God, and be ashamed of our meanness and carelessness.

For fading and temporal goods no labour is thought superfluous, or too great, and for the gaining of all good things anything, no matter how trifling and trivial, is deemed intolerable.

For a vile and trifling gain dangers that threaten life are freely surmounted by many merchants in the world; and for eternal happiness, if anything seems burdensome or troublesome to nature, it cannot be endured.

For a booty that is worthless and only secured after much hardship, many soldiers fearlessly expose themselves to the blows of the enemy, and receive many wounds; and for the crown of glory scarcely do we ever resist the devil and the allurements of the flesh.

5. O would to God, that we opened our eyes, and grew wise and understood.

Could pain be mingled with the joys of Heaven, assuredly all the Saints would weep and mourn from their very souls, for not having served God in greater fervour, and merited a more ample reward, whilst it was still time.

One degree of glory infinitely surpasseth the value of all human wealth.

One drop of that most precious nectar exceeds an ocean of earthly pleasure.

If ever for one instant the beautifulness of the reward to be conferred on any good work whatsoever, were to appear to the eyes of the damned, they would forthwith feel no sorrow at such cruel torments, and hell would appear to have become like unto paradise.

If then we show that we slight such surpassing and magnificent rewards, we are truly blind and foolish.

6. Let us learn, therefore, from the children of this world, diligence, fortitude, patience, and industry, that we may lay up for ourselves in time, whilst we may, the riches of an imperishable reward.

Every plan must be carefully thought of by which we may derive the greatest possible advantage from our life.

Every opportunity must be diligently sought after, waited for, and embraced, in which any chance of merit may be seized upon.

All the powers of our body and soul are to be cheerfully lavished upon such an affair, though we should add but one degree of glory to our future reward.

7. We must never say: *I have enough, I have merited enough, I am quite contented if I ever attain eternal life.*

This is what the imperfect and imprudent say, who do not understand the greatness of the Divine reward.

Thus speak the ungrateful and proud, who by not thinking of increasing the merit of their glory, seem to slight that very glory itself, and prove that they love God but very little.

Thus speak the carnal-minded and the close adherents of the world, who loathe

spiritual goods, because, being full of inordinate desires, they cannot taste and see
how sweet the Lord is.

8. But do thou hearken to the counsel
of our Lord, which thou shouldst ever
follow: *Lay up for yourselves treasures in
Heaven.*

Hearken to that precept of the Lord,
which is to be kept with fear and trembling: *Trade till I come.*

Hearken also to the sentence and judgment of the Lord, that should be deeply
·imprinted in thy soul: *Blessed are they that
hunger and thirst after justice, for they shall
have their fill.*

If thou hearken to these with docility,
ponder them with attention, and carry
them into practice with a good will, behold
the Lord shall come in the day, which He
hath appointed, and shall give thee the
kiss of peace and perpetual love, and shall
place thee over all His goods, saying:
Enter into the joy of thy Lord.

CHAPTER IX.

That we ought to be grateful to God for the Blessings
which we have received.

1. SON, be mindful of the great benefits
that thou hast received; and often think
how thou mayest use them for My glory.

For thine is not a trifling debt, nor can
it be discharged without great diligence
and constancy.

Does it then seem to thee a small thing,
that I vouchsafed to create thee from nothing, and came to redeem thee, when thou
hadst perished.

I have loved thee with an everlasting love;
loved thee, I say, who hast so often slighted
My love, and miserably defiled My image.

Still thou hast not overcome My love
and patience.

And I have said: *Behold I stand at the
door and knock: Open to Me, My beloved, for
My head is full of dew, and My locks of the
drops of the nights.*

2. Whatever thou hast, is Mine; for from My liberality all things have pro-ceeded.

Whatever thou canst do, thou canst do it only by Me; for *without Me, you can do nothing.*

Whatever thou dost hope for, can be obtained by Me alone, for I am the Lord of armies and the King of glory.

Cast thine eyes upon the heavens and the earth, and all creatures; I am in all of them, and I labour in them all for thy advantage, that thou mayest serve Me with joy.

Consider thyself, whom I have created to My own image, called to My Church, strengthened with the word of life, snatched from the dangers of hell, chosen for My own temple, nourished with My own flesh, cleansed with My blood, destined for un-speakable glory with the holy Angels.

3. Come, then, My son; *Forget not the kindness of thy surety: for He hath given His life for thee.*

I have done much for thee, suffered much; and still I ask not for much in return : *My son, give Me thy heart,* and I am content.

Acknowledge with humility that thou hast received everything without any merit on thy part, and that, hitherto, thou hast been a useless servant, and I am content.

Let me work freely in thee, and concerning thee, whatever is expedient for thee, and I am content.

Use My benefits to good account, and I am content.

For this is My will concerning thee, that thou shouldst make Me a return for My benefits, and thus permit thyself to be loaded with fresh benefits.

Why then dost thou resist My generosity? why dost thou force Me by your negligence to depart?

Why dost thou not look to the poverty of thy soul, and why dost thou scarce leave Me a place for My treasures?

4. O Lord, I am confounded and ashamed,

5

that Thou art more ready to give than I to receive.

Expand the heart of Thy servant, warm me with the fire of Thy charity, make me wholly according to Thy heart.

I give Thee thanks, O Lord, for having vouchsafed to bring me out of nothing, to empty Thyself for me, to be tortured even unto death for me.

I give Thee thanks for having generously decreed to foster me with Thy grace, to fill me with a thousand good things, and even, when I was Thy enemy, to be the first to love me.

I give Thee thanks for not having rejected me for my ingratitude, nor cast me into hell, but for having, on the contrary, often salutarily reproached me in my conscience, punished me as a friend, and urged me on to better gifts.

5. What return shall I make unto Thee, O Lord, for all that Thou hast done to me? Behold, I have nothing; because whatever I have, yea, whatever I am, is Thine, and came from Thee.

Deign, O Lord, to receive me for Thy willing slave, for I desire to resign myself wholly into Thy hands, that I may walk in the way of Thy justifications, according to what is well-pleasing to Thy holy will.

Is it then a great thing for me to serve Thee with all my powers, who art the Lord of all?

Should it be a hard thing to renounce the consolations of the senses and men, and to labour even unto exhaustion and death, when Thou hast deigned to pour out all Thy blood for me?

Can it be a burden to deny my evil desires, and hate my own soul, in order to please Thee, after Thou hast snatched my soul from the lower hell and eternal fires?

6. Such is my desire, such my resolve; help me, O Lord, I beseech Thee, with Thy grace, that I may know the unspeakable price of Thy benefits.

Show me how great are the things which Thou hast given; how much greater what Thou art going to give.

Imprint them all in my heart, that the
·remembrance of the benefits which I have
received, and the expectation of those to
come, may unceasingly strengthen me·in
Thy holy service, and be to me a constant
spur to labour strenuously.

CHAPTER X.

That Persecutions and Calumnies should move us to a
more zealous Pursuit of Perfection.

1. ARISE, O Lord, to my aid; delay not,
for the waters of tribulations have entered
even into my soul; comfort Thy servants,
and scatter those that afflict them.

Be not unmindful, O Lord, of our affliction; for Thee are we in labour, for Thee
are we mortified all the day.

We are reputed as sheep for the slaughter;
save us, O Lord, because we have put our
trust in Thee.

2. Son, *if they have persecuted Me, they will*

also persecute you; for the disciple is not above his master.

Have I not foretold it to thee ? what else canst thou expect from those that are placed in iniquity, and under the yoke of the devil, but that they will persecute the servants of God, and the enemies of the devil ?

If you were of the world, the world would love its own. But because you are not of the world, therefore the world hateth you. Be glad and rejoice, for your reward is very great in Heaven.

Cease, then, thy complaints, son ; if thou thinkest rightly, thou shouldst assuredly give thanks ; for it is a great benefit to suffer tribulation and affliction for Me, and on account of Me.

3. He that endureth tribulation and per-secution for My name let him glory in them ; for *he that suffereth with Me, shall also reign with Me.*

And I am wont to correct and chastise in this world whomsoever I love, that he

5*

may not be condemned with the world; but after being tried by fire and water may come to refreshment with Me.

Tribulation and persecution are most profitable to My servants; for by them they make not only easy, but great and rapid progress.

For they that meet with tribulation from the world, and find no comfort from men, are wont to fly to Me for refuge with great confidence, alacrity, and devotion.

4. They are wont, too, to inspect their life more narrowly, and to correct and cut off with great diligence whatever can offend their neighbours.

And they are mutually united to one another by a more fervent charity, they pray more devoutly, live in greater meekness, and employ greater energy in furnishing themselves with spiritual arms.

They fast, are humbled, purified from earthly affections, cling to meditations on heavenly things.

They keep away from vain conversa-

tions, speak on useful and spiritual subjects, and become better suited to assist
their neighbour.

And hence I permit My beloved servants
to be in tribulation, to be hated, and de-
nounced as evil.

5. If, then, thou wilt please Me, seek not
impatiently to be freed from thy difficulties; 'for it is well to be purged in this
world;' but leaving everything else to Me,
seek solely to bear thyself courageously in
difficulties.

Pray for those that persecute and afflict
thee and thy brethren, in order that they
too may find salvation; do good to them
as much as thou canst, for thus did I also
act.

If they justly reprehend anything in
thee, correct it with solicitude; if they do
thee an injury, bear with it for My name.

See that thou grow not cowardly, and
turn timid in My service.

Cease not from works of charity, despise contumely, scorn reports, fear not the

threats of men, and strive strenuously to promote My glory.

Say to thy soul: Behold God alone is my hope and my refuge; *He is my God, I will hope in Him.*

If armies in camp should stand against me, my heart shall not fear. If a battle should rise up against me, in this will I be confident.

What thanks do I owe the Lord for having deigned to admit me amongst the soldiers of His cross!

Would that I deserved to be inebriated with the chalice of my Lord, and to resist even unto blood!

6. He that has such dispositions, is a spectacle to God, and the Angels, and men, and whatever happeneth he shall not be moved.

But he that still seeks anxiously for the vain friendships of man, and desireth to be highly esteemed, easily fails and proves cowardly in tribulations.

Such a one secures ignominy and misfortune to himself where others more fervent and courageous acquire great glory and merit.

Wherefore thou must be on thy guard, son, and solicitously advance forward in order that thou mayest be entirely free from stain, and pleasing to the divine eye in everything.

7. For the rest, be of good courage: *Are not two sparrows sold for a farthing? and not one of them shall fall on the ground without your Father. Fear not, therefore; better are you than many sparrows; in the regeneration not a hair of your head shall perish.*

Then all these temporal things, whether they have been prosperous or adverse, will be past, and a crown shall be given to the victors in a blessed eternity.

Then he, that has endured more tribulations for Me, shall be glorified the more.

For it is the will of My Father and My will, that the more one has resembled Me in patience, the more like unto Me, he shall be in the crown of victory.

CHAPTER XI.

That it is only by the Pursuit of Perfection that we can assuage the Evils of this Life.

1. THINK as much as thou wilt; thou wilt find no true solace in human things for the tumults and miseries of this fickle and deplorable life.

Though thou runnest over every place, and attemptest every means, thou wilt not acquire peace; yea, the sense of thy evils will be more bitter after, than before, a useless remedy.

Look at worldlings; they live in the greatest misery, even though they seek after happiness with the greatest efforts.

They gather consolation on every side and still are neither happy nor satisfied; because all the consolations of this world are vanity, and from not intimately considering themselves, they see not how great is their error.

2. Keep far away from these; seek to please God, look after thy own perfection; for it will soothe all thy evils far more easily, than all the delights and riches of the world.

If thou gain thy perfection in the state of life which thou hast embraced, nothing in this world will be able to disturb thee.

Not poverty, not the scorn of men, not disease, not stripes, not prison, not temptations, not death itself.

For he, that attaineth to perfection, fears them not, nay, not even considers them evils, but blessings; because he sees that Christ has gone before us by His example in all these things. And it cannot be that what Christ both embraced Himself, and taught us to embrace, should not be good.

The nearer thou art to perfection, the less wilt thou fear them; nay, little by little thou wilt even desire them, and glory willingly in them with the Apostles.

3. What then can disturb or sadden thee, if these very things become to thee an occasion of joy and exultation.

O truly blessed even in this world is the religious, that is fervent and zealous for his own perfection !

O truly unspeakable delight of virtue, that not only absorbs, but renders sweet, the bitterness arising from temporal losses !

If ever thou hast been fervent, thou knowest assuredly how true all this is, and how far beyond all description of words is this happiness.

4. See how many good religious rejoice in tribulations, congratulate themselves on persecutions, and take pleasure in their infirmities, and thank God for them. ·

How spontaneous are these joys! how true the peace! how sincere the gladness!

For such, by the goodness and grace of God, is the working and reward of virtue in those that love perfection.

Let then this intrinsic force of virtue, so great and wonderful, move thee to a great love of virtue.   ·

Whatever adversity may occur, it will be easily smoothed down, assuaged and sweetened by love of perfection alone.

For a good and pure conscience is ever tranquil, ever rejoicing, and ever happy.

5. But on the contrary, if ever thou hast lived tepidly, remember how hard and distasteful everything became.

Not only thou couldst not soothe the adversities that befell thee, but thou didst make them still more severe, and by many other ways didst bring crosses and trials on thyself.

No one in the world is more unhappy than a tepid and negligent religious; for he has no share in the joys of either the world or Heaven, and thus is often exposed to sadness.

On the contrary, he has many burdens to bear which seculars have not; and because he cannot bear them, he ceases not to repine and be oppressed with difficulties.

And what is still harder for the wretched man is, that he cannot attribute the blame of his faults to any one but himself; for he sees that he is himself the cause of his affliction and pain.

6

6. O how great a good is perfection! Even though its reward is reserved in the kingdom of God, until after death, still it is not wholly deferred.

Perfection is a comfort in adversities, a pleasure in sadness, a treasure in misfortunes.

Perfection is the source of all joy and consolation, a pure, abundant, and unfailing source.

Perfection is, as it were, a very high region, where neither clouds nor tempests arise, nor winds rage, nor anything unpleasant happens; but everything is in rest, tranquility, and calm.

Perfection makes us experience with what truth Christ preached, when he said: *Take up My yoke upon you; for My yoke is sweet and My burden light.*

Chapter XII.

That it is necessary to be prepared by the Pursuit of
Perfection for dying happily.

1. CAST thine eyes around thee upon all
creatures, and consider their perpetual state
of transition and instability.

What was yesterday, is not, or is different
to-day; all things pass away, and thou also
with them.

*For we have not here a lasting city, but we
seek one that is to come,* that is, the heavenly
Jerusalem, in which everything good is
perfect and lasting.

Why then art thou solicitous about
earthly ease and comforts; which must
either leave thee during life, or at least be
left by thee at death?

Seek rather the means of rising at once
to great sanctity, and acquiring eternal
consolations.

Behold death will come, and will not
tarry long; if, by the study of perfection,

thou hast diligently prepared thyself for the journey of eternity, the necessity of dying, that will then press upon thee, will bring no anguish to thy soul.

2. O what consolation in death do the servants of God feel, that have always lived in readiness to die!

What hope does the remembrance of their past life and the testimony of an unsullied conscience afford them!

For from their having sedulously followed the Divine inspirations, and always studied to please God more and more, they feel that God is their friend, and they have no ground for exciting fear in their soul.

And as people, that have already prepared everything that is necessary and useful for their voyage, they hasten to enter into the rest, from which they have been bound to be absent so long.

For who would not be glad and exult at the approach of the end of all misery, the beginning of perfect beatitude, and entire security from all sin?

3. But unless thou have prepared thyself all thy life, thou wilt not feel how desirable and blessed a thing it is to depart from this world.

If thy heart seek its rest now in any creature, it will then be torn away with difficulty from it, and turned towards God.

If now thou bewail not thy sins, and do not deeds of penance, thou wilt fear the approach of death, and be terror-stricken at the thought of the just judgment of God.

If thou have taken but little care of thy perfection, thy conscience will reproach thee, the necessity of rendering thy account will give thee anguish, and the expectation of punishment terrify thee.

Why then dost thou neglect to look to thyself? Why put off from day to day the care of thy amendment?

4. If thou wert now at the point of death, certainly thou wouldst not be displeased at having frequently made use of scourges, haircloths, fasts and prayers; but thou wouldst of a certainty grieve exceedingly

6*

for not having resisted the inordinate tendencies of thy passions.

Thou wouldst not receive any harm from having been humble, kind, patient, a lover of labour, obedient, and devout; but much from having reckoned such things of little value, and scarcely thought of conforming thy life to religious discipline.

What, therefore, thou wouldst hereafter wish to have done, do it now, lest, perchance, afterwards thou have to lament in vain the fewness of thy merits, and the multitude of thy sins.

This life is the time of satisfaction and merit; at death how dost thou know that thou wilt even be in thy senses?

How wilt thou in a few days make good the loss of so many years, which thou hast lived in tepidity, and heaped up straw about thy soul for burning?

And if death seize upon thee, at the hour when thou dost least expect it, thou that couldst in this life so easily have satisfied thy debt to God, wilt then have to pay it off to the last farthing.

And even if a long life still remain to thee, thou wilt never rejoice at having deferred thy repentance; and moreover, grieve as thou wilt, thou shalt never turn to advantage the time that has been lost.

5. *Blessed is the servant, whom when his Lord shall come, and shall knock at the door, He shall find on the watch.*

Blessed is his life, although he endureth much from men; because he enjoys true peace, who is always prepared to answer to the call of his God. ·

Blessed is his death, though the devil rage then still more furiously, knowing that he has but little time: for *precious in the sight of the Lord is the death of His Saints.*

· Blessed is his eternity, in which the Lord shall inebriate him with a torrent of delight, and fill him with the unspeakable sweetness of the heavenly manna.

And hence it was that the Saints often used to congratulate themselves on having to die, and not only feared not death, but held it as a great blessing.

But they, that strive not to become holy, live in sadness, load themselves with sins, die in anxiety, and justly stand in dread of the secret judgments of God.

CHAPTER XIII.

That the Eternity of the Rewards of Heaven is often to be compared with the Labours of this mortal Life.

1. SUCH is the weakness of human nature, that each one prefers resting upon what is well done, to advancing boldly to what is yet to be performed.

It pleaseth men to have a good witness of themselves; and consequently whenever they perform a good action, they keep it constantly before their eyes, congratulate themselves upon it, and however small it may be, always consider it something great.

But if they have done aught ill, or are wanting in some good quality, they instantly turn away their eyes, that they may not be pained, or vex themselves from such consideration.

They are truly foolish and blind, that seem to themselves already rich enough, and think that they have already laboured sufficiently for eternal life.

Are they then more holy than the Apostle St. Paul? And yet he, though fully aware that he had laboured more than the rest of the Apostles, as he himself has testified, believed that he could not indulge in idleness.

Hear what he saith: *Brethren, I do not count myself to have apprehended, but one thing I do: forgetting the things that are behind, and stretching forth myself to those that are before, I press towards the mark, to the prize of the supernal vocation of God in Christ Jesus.*

2. Do thou also dwell in thought on this eternal reward: think on what thou art going to do for so great a good, and forget what thou thinkest thyself to have hitherto done well.

For if thou compare the good deeds that thou hast performed with the glory that is to come, they will seem to thee almost nothing, and in a manner wholly vanish out of sight.

Know also that much of what thou perchance didst believe to be good was bad, and deserved punishment rather than reward.

For man knoweth not whether he be worthy of love or hatred; and therefore, however much thou hast done, thou art not secure.

3. O that thou wouldst frequently turn over in mind the thought of a blessed eternity ! Assuredly, such a thought would excite thee to undergo labours, stimulate thee to abandon thy own ease, and urge thee to value nothing but virtue.

For by virtue alone is purchased that inestimable joy, that ineffable happiness, which *eye hath not seen, nor ear heard, neither hath it entered into the heart of man.*

Thou wouldst then understand how little, or nothing, is the good performed by thee, and thou wouldst grieve most bitterly at having lost many degrees of glory by thy negligence in making progress.

Nor would then any labour appear grievous to thee, endured, or yet to be endured, in overcoming thy vices; on the contrary, it would be a subject of the greatest pleasure to one who knew that every victory over vice *worketh for us an eternal weight of glory.*

4. Why, I pray, art thou sorrowful in this fight against sensuality? Why dost thou complain of contempt? Why dost thou murmur at an occasion of suffering that is presented to thee?

Certainly pagans and infidels, and all that have no hope may well be sad; but by what right is a servant of God overpowered with sadness in labours and crosses, to which the kingdom of Heaven is promised?

But, alas! just as worldlings rejoice at most wicked things, when they should rather tremble at the vengeance of God that hangs over them; so, contrariwise, imperfect religious are often sad at those things for which they should rejoice beyond measure.

Hath not Christ our Lord taught us to glory in the troubles of this life, to rejoice and be glad in them, because our reward in Heaven should be very great?

But if thou scarce ever think of this reward, it is not surprising that thou seekest repose, avoidest inconveniences, lovest the things of the earth, hatest humiliations, and neglectest entirely the study of thy perfection.

5. A religious meets with many difficulties, over which nature alone cannot gain the victory.

Neither human reasonings, nor the uprightness of the deed, nor the praises or reproofs of men, nor any other motive of temporal gain gives sufficient inducement.

If thou think on these alone, thou wilt either do no good at all, or do it remissly; if thou begin it, thou wilt not long persevere in it; nor even if thou finish it, wilt thou have peace; and what is still more deplorable, thou wilt lose thy labour, and undergo to thy own loss the hardships of virtue.

But if thou keep thy thoughts fixed upon eternal happiness, and compare its greatness with the smallness of the labour, its eternity with the moment of tribulation, thou wilt always have a useful incentive to virtue.

Then it will not grieve thee to suffer tribulation, but to be without it, and repose, and not labour, will displease thee.

6. Say then to thyself: Now is the time for working, now is the time for laying up merit, now is the time for sowing. .

If I sow plentifully now, then I shall reap in the greatest abundance; but if I am loath to sow, then my soul will be empty. If now I employ in traffic my talent, I shall receive usury; but if I bury my talent in the earth, I shall be cast out into the exterior darkness.

The more I suffer now, the more un-

7

utterable will be my rejoicing then; but if I refuse to suffer, God will sift me in devouring flames.

It is not a great thing for me to serve God with diligence; but it is something great and wonderful, that God should promise such a recompense for this my service.

Much wisdom is not needed to prompt me to labour at my perfection; rather it is a folly beyond belief for me not to toil with the greatest constancy after perfection, when so great a reward is proposed to me.

Let then the thought of this most perfect happiness be to thee a daily incentive.

Suffer not thy body to complain of too much fatigue; but renew its forces from supernatural treasures.

Love not to see now what is beautiful and great; conquer thyself and thou shalt be able to see the wonders of God with greater clearness.

Seek not to enjoy now great peace; labour in patience, and thou shalt obtain eternal delights.

Fear not now to be humbled and trodden under foot by men; but imitate Christ, and He Himself shall deck thee with nobility above all comprehension.

Blush not to use mean garments, and to manifest other signs of poverty, and thou shalt enjoy all the treasures of Heaven for ever.

For behold, *It is sown a natural body, it shall rise a spiritual body; it is sown in corruption, it shall rise in incorruption; it is sown in dishonour, it shall rise in glory: it is sown in weakness, it shall rise in power.*

CHAPTER XIV.

That Love of God should draw us to Perfection.

1. LOVE is indeed a great thing, and great is the power of love. He that loves cannot remain idle, but is either searching out some means of pleasing his beloved, or working for his beloved, or speaking of his beloved, or conversing familiarly with his beloved.

Love drew God down to thee, and forced Him to become man, that He might heap fresh benefits upon thee; nor did He become man only, but He would suffer and die for thy sake, and be eaten by thee.

Why then dost thou say that thou lovest God, and yet doest not what thou knowest to be most pleasing to Him?

If thou didst truly love God, thou wouldst diligently cleanse thy soul from vices, and adorn thyself with virtues, in order that thou mightest daily appear more worthy of love in the eyes of God.

Thou wouldst avoid many distractions, and strive to have God present and glorify Him in every word and deed.

Thou wouldst with all care seek the solitude of thy mind to treat with God familiarly, and intimately unite thyself to Him.

2. He that loves is not sad, when he suffers some loss; refuses not suffering when it is presented to him, and is not worn out with fatigue, when he has to labour.

A true and sincere love desireth love alone for its reward, and despiseth everything else.

If the consideration of heavenly things grow insipid to thee, when spiritual consolation faileth, thou art convicted of loving thy own consolation more than the will of God.

If thou recoil from labours, and be lukewarm in promoting the glory of God, thou lovest thine own ease more than God Himself.

7*

If thou be still solicitous about earthly goods, about the opinions of men, and worldly glory, behold, thou hast not yet given thy whole heart to God, but kept it for thyself and the world.

Love for God excludes affection for sensible things, and suffers us not to be moved by them, except for the sake of God, inasmuch as they are from God, and lead to God.

3. To him that loveth, everything is insipid, that relates not to his beloved; and if it were possible, the lover would wish to to go out of himself, and transfer himself wholly into his beloved, that thus he might be perfectly one with him.

And because he cannot do this, he desires to be in his company, endeavours to have the same sentiments, rejoices to be the same in will, the same in words, the same in action, the same in suffering.

Give God then this proof of love, that He too may love thee the more; see that thou conform thyself to God in all things.

Bend thy will to the wishes of thy Superiors; so shalt thou do the will of God, and be pleasing to Him.

Obey with all promptness and greatness of soul the inspirations of divine grace, and God will love thee.

Follow the examples of Christ in true and internal humility, charity and patience, and God the Father will love thee as the brother of His only-begotten Son, Christ Jesus, in whom He is well pleased.

For Christ our Lord was always most dear to His Father, precisely because He did not do His own will, but the will of Him that sent Him.

4. O how coldly do we love God, that scarcely ever think seriously of our own progress!

Would not a son love his father with a very little love, if he would not hearken to his counsels, and continually withheld himself from all familiar intercourse with him?

An affectionate son cannot long be absent

from his father and deprived of his conversation; and whenever he knows the will or
desire of his father, he endeavours to carry
it out forthwith.

But such, alas! is not our life; for although we know that God takes delight in
our denying ourselves, it scarcely makes
any impression on us, and we still love
ourselves inordinately.

Although we know that humble obedience and simplicity are well pleasing in the
sight of God, we often resist in our interior
the will of our Superiors and murmur in
our heart.

Although we have learned how acceptable to God are prayer and compunction,
still we prefer to be distracted from day to
day, and scarce give a thought to our perfection.

5. Alas! when shall we begin to love
God more fervently? If, however much
we love, our love is nothing, and *we are
useless servants*, how great, I ask, should be
our confusion at loving so little?

When shall we be able to say with Christ, at least in some measure: *My meat is to do the will of Him that sent me?* and, *I do always the things that please Him?*

Let us therefore leave all things for the sake of God, and with other things let us leave ourselves.

Let us conform our judgment to the Scripture, our will to obedience; let us despise what is temporal, and cling to what is of the spirit, let us often lift ourselves up to God Himself.

Let our study be to study what is more perfect: if we fail, let us be sorry for it; if we have an opportunity of practising virtue, let us not pass it unheeded; let us take care to carry off each day some little victory over our vices.

Chapter XV.

That the Mystery of Predestination should excite us
to the Pursuit of Perfection.

1. *Whom He foreknew, He also predesti-*
nated to be made conformable to the image of
His Son, that He might be the first-born
amongst many brethren.

If any one will enter into the kingdom of
Heaven, he must be conformable to Christ
in virtues; unless thou become the brother
of Christ by a good life, God will not receive thee into the glory of His children.

See then thy present state, and if thou
art little solicitous to imitate Christ, be
filled with fear: for *the judgments of God*
are a great abyss.

Let theologians dispute, as much as they
will, about the hidden mystery of predestination; but do thou say to thyself: *Ought*
not Christ to have suffered these things, and so
to enter into His glory ?

And again: *They that are Christ's have crucified their flesh with its vices and concupiscences.*

And again: *If we suffer, we shall also reign with Him;* and, *If any one have not the Spirit of Christ, he is none of His.*

2. This, this is what we ought both to know and often think on, and not the depth of the mysteries of God.

Of this indeed we shall have to render an account; and for this reason it is that these things are so clearly set forth in the Scriptures.

If we cling firmly to this, to have been ignorant of the hidden things of the mysteries of God will do us no harm; nor indeed will God question us on the subtlety of our reasoning, but on the perfection with which we have lived.

God would not have the hidden mystery of predestination known to men, lest perchance they should abuse such knowledge.

For it is of service to us to have no security of this affair, since we are by this means more humble and diligent.

Wherefore St. Paul said: *With fear and trembling, work out your salvation.* And St. Peter: *Labour the more, that by good works you may make sure your calling and election.*

3. For by good works we may with great probability conjecture what will befall us in the next life; and yet, in such a measure, that we cannot ever be wholly free from fear and trembling.

Here then is the very best proof of being predestined, and one the least uncertain of all: to be employed with diligence in the service of God, and to labour seriously to attain to the perfection which Christ has proposed.

For He saith: *Blessed are they that hunger and thirst after justice, for they shall have their fill.*

But if one grow torpid in the service of God, and care not to make progress, he may well be filled with a most lively fear; for *cursed is he that doeth the work of the Lord deceitfully.*

And, in fact, the servant that is called

wicked in the Gospel, is recorded to have been thrust into the exterior darkness, because he would not make profit, and returned to the Lord no more than he had received to traffic with.

4. Let us, then, prepare this consolation for ourselves both in life and death, that thus we may with reason confide in our future lot.

Let us imitate Christ now: *But He will reform the body of our lowness made like to the body of His glory.*

Let us learn to obey God with love, who calls us to perfection, that we may deserve to be His sons for ever: *But if sons, then heirs also.*

This thought will make us, with the grace of God, scarce ever feel any labour, and become stronger in temptations.

For there is nothing so bitter that will not become agreeable, when sweetened with so much hope, and nothing so burdensome, that will not be made light in the presence of such and so great a reward.

8

CHAPTER XVI.

That Love of our Neighbour should excite us to Perfection.

1. *My little children*, saith St. John, *let us not love in word, nor in tongue, but in deed and in truth.*

If thou dost truly love thy neighbour and desire to be useful to him, it is not enough to preach the word of God, and fulfill the other duties of instructing, advising and consoling.

Although thou perform all these things, if thou wilt not direct thy labours to thyself, that so thou mayest become a fitting instrument for the Divine glory, thou dost not yet love in deed and in truth.

Tell me; if any one should try to cut with a hammer, or paint with a saw, would he not labour in vain?

So, too, thou also art useless to procure the amendment of others, so long as thou carest not for thy own advancement.

And hence thy voice is *like sounding brass and a tinkling cymbal;* and thy charity is in word, not in deed; for thou omittest the deeds that thy neighbour stands most in need of.

2. Great, indeed, is the supply of ministers of God. But, alas! how little is the fruit that follows the preaching of many! Would that we were fewer and better!

Every day almost we inveigh against vice, praise virtue, demonstrate by words the necessity of good works; and still the world appears to grow worse every day. How is it, then, that our labour is without fruit? because our life agreeth not well with the dignity of our ministry.

The word of the Lord is a double-edged sword; but unless God teach us internally the art of combating, not only we shall not overpower the vices of the world and the powers of the devil, but we shall strike ourselves through our want of skill.

But how shall God teach thee internally, unless thou prepare a place for him, and dispose thyself to hear His voice by recollection of mind and devotion?

3. He that converseth often with God in prayer, and strives to increase in perfection, knows how to gain great victories, whenever he employs this spiritual sword.

At times one fervent man has reformed and brought back to God, whole cities and kingdoms, after many others had attempted it in vain; in the same manner as Jonas alone converted all the Ninivites.

Think on the great fruit, which St. Paul and the other Apostles reaped in every part of the world from their preaching! but meanwhile, although full of the Holy Ghost, they laboured at their own self-denial.

They spared not themselves, prayed fervently, and thought it all joy to fall into various temptations.

Their light shone before men, and because they saw that their works were good, they glorified their Father who is in Heaven.

They feared not persecutions, but met

them with undaunted courage, and often *went away rejoicing that they were accounted worthy to suffer reproach for the name of Jesus.*

4. Consult histories : thou wilt find that devout and simple men have been of much greater service to the world, than learned men, without devotion, and puffed up with their knowledge.

For the world is not converted *in the persuasive words of human wisdom,* but in the power of the cross of Christ.

How then shall he, that loveth not the cross, be able to invite others at all profitably to the following of the cross.

Let us not delude ourselves : *It is the spirit that quickeneth ; the flesh profiteth nothing. If the salt lose its savour, wherewith shall it be salted? It is good for nothing any more, but to be cast out and to be trodden on by men.*

And hence perchance it is, that many laugh at us and say : *These men are clouds without water, which are carried about by winds.*

8*

For though we should be spiritual men, they perceive many defects in us, which are of very great injury to our ministry.

5. Unless then thou cleanse thyself from all vices with very great diligence, and strive even to increase in virtues, in vain will be thy exertions to procure the salvation of thy neighbour.

And though God, through His tender commiseration for men, may grant some fruit, still thou wilt hinder that fruit from being more abundant.

Unless thou pay serious attention to thy own sanctification, thou wilt not promote the greater glory of God, but the greater the negligence, the more thou wilt seem to wish to contract and lessen that glory.

O conduct unworthy of a religious man! O mournful indolence and detestable cowardice!

Behold, God has deigned to enrol thee amongst His soldiers, and to provide thee with spiritual arms; has He not done so, in order that thou shouldst learn by a victory over thy vices to free others also from their vices?

Great is the honour, great the favour of being a soldier of Christ; but greater is the confusion and greater the crime to betray the cause of Christ, after having received arms from Him.

Great is the dignity, wonderful the vocation to snatch souls from the snares of the devil; but great also are the burden and the obligation of making a return for so great a benefit.

Sublime is the ministry, *and the most divine of all divine things to co-operate with God in the salvation of souls;* but it requires almost divine men, to wit, men that have put off the old Adam, and put on the new man, Christ, *who is over all things, God blessed for ever.*

CHAPTER XVII.

That the Remembrance of our Sins should excite us to Perfection.

1. IF thou hast ever sinned, let the remembrance of thy sins be at least a motive for resolving to serve God more fervently, and to rise to higher perfection.

And since the devil succeeded in drawing thee from God by sin, see now how thou mayest confound the devil by the recollection of thy sins, and draw nigh unto God.

Consider how foolish thou hast been in wishing to resist God; how ungrateful, in making use of His benefits to injure thy benefactor.

See how thou hast defiled thyself by sinning, what ignominy and torments thou hast deserved, how kindly God has called thee and waited for thee.

2. He that thinks over these things with

attention and ponders them well, finds great cause and matter for humility.

Gather then this fruit of humility from the remembrance of thy past life, and thy past sin will not only do thee no harm, but spur thee on to virtue.

Thou wilt not despise a mean habit, spare food, and a poor cell, if thou call to mind, that thou hast deserved to dwell for ever in devouring flames.

It is but just that he, who is conscious of having lain for a long time in the power of devils, should allow himself to be trodden under the feet of all.

To be very humble in his words and deeds, may well become one that knows, that he has been the enemy of God, and knows not that he has since truly entered into His favour again.

3. Thou mayest also gather another fruit from the memory of thy sins, namely, a great hatred of thyself.

For it is not fitting to lavish caresses on thy body, after it has become an instrument of sin.

The body must be reduced to slavery, to prevent its ever again fighting against God; yea, it must be forced to serve God in spite of itself.

Listen to the Apostle: *As you have yielded your members to serve uncleanness and iniquity unto iniquity, so now yield your members to serve justice unto sanctification.*

For in truth the honour, which was taken from God by sin, must be rendered back; and because all thy services will never be able to equal the grievousness of the injury, know that thou must never desist from repairing that injury.

Chastise then thy body, keep a guard over thy eyes, bridle thy tongue, resist thy appetite, mortify the touch, and all the members by which thou hast sinned.

Deny thy external senses, not only that they may not injure thee, but also in punishment for past liberty.

Renounce thy own will, not only that it may not rise in rebellion, but also because he that has once dared to resist the will of God, deserves never to do his own will.

4. Would to God, that thou wouldst often weigh these things well, and treasure them in thy heart with a most intimate feeling of sorrow! How quickly wouldst thou become better!

Thou wouldst quickly understand, how patient thou shouldst be, how obedient, how pure, how fervent.

And though it be never lawful to rejoice at sin committed, still thou couldst truly say: O happy fault, the remembrance of which furnishes me with so great an occasion of merit!

For God permitted Peter also to fall, that he might have greater cause for humility and making progress.

St. Paul, too, and other Saints, were most vehemently stirred by the remembrance of their sins to serve God daily with greater fervour.

For he, that has ever been the servant of sin, should labour with the greater ardour, either to repair the injury he has done himself, or to redeem the time that has been lost, or to glorify the more by the rest of his life the God whom he has dishonoured.

5. The more grievous have been thy sins, the more solicitous shouldst thou be about good works, according to the words of the Scripture: *Return, as you had deeply revolted.*

The longer God bore with thee, when thou wast sinning, the more ardently shouldst thou now love Him.

Dost thou not see from this, how He loved thee in spite of thy ingratitude?

He could have given thee over to be punished by devils, and yet he would not.

He knew that thou wouldst sin anew, and again abuse His goodness, and yet He spared thee; He had rather endure the offence, than condemn thee to eternal fire.

Therefore give Him thanks for so much patience, and, keeping in mind the memory of so great a favour, stir thyself up to love Him.

Let justice superabound, where iniquity has abounded: say to God: *Wash me yet*

*more from my iniquity, and cleanse me from
my sin; for I know my iniquity, and my sin
is always before me.*

And because whatever thou dost do, is
but little, take care that others also may
learn from thee to glorify God; and thus
thou shalt make fuller atonement for the
injury offered to God.

Therefore make a firm resolution, and
say with the Prophet: *I will teach the unjust Thy ways, and the wicked shall be converted to Thee.*

CHAPTER XVIII.

That the Assistance of Grace renders the Way of Perfection easy.

1. THOUGH thou art still very imperfect,
be not cast down; provided thy will is
sincere, thou also shalt arrive at perfection.

Regard not the strength of nature, but
that of grace; not the weakness of the
flesh, but the power of God.

9

For thou hast not to enter upon the way of sanctity by thyself, but in the company of Christ, who is prepared to assist thee, if thou wilt not resist Him.

I am the vine, He says, *you the branches; he that abideth in Me, and I in him, the same beareth much fruit.*

He, that trusteth in himself, does indeed quickly fall, and rush into the abyss; because he leaneth on a broken reed; and hence St. Peter denied Christ.

But he, that distrusts himself and commits himself to the care of Divine grace, goeth in security and attaineth to perfection, even though many arduous and difficult things stand in his way.

2. The way of perfection doubtless is hard for human imbecility; and therefore the Scripture says: *Strive to enter by the narrow gate.* But listen to St. Paul: *I can do all things in Him who strengtheneth me.*

Christ our Lord also hath said: *Take up My yoke upon you;* but He added: *For My yoke is sweet, and My burden light.*

He hath said too: *The kingdom of Heaven suffereth violence, and the violent bear it away,* and other similar things. But listen to the Apostle again, as he says: *I exceedingly abound with joy in all my tribulations.*

Interrogate holy and devout religious, that have given themselves wholly to God, and thou wilt understand how easy all these things become by the grace of God.

Learn to follow the movements of grace, and thou wilt know how easy is the law of Christ; for it will carry thee rather than thou it.

For the law of Christ is the law of love and grace; and if it seem difficult to any one, it is not certainly so to one that loves Christ, and receives with diligence the visitation of grace.

3. Give then an entrance to God; prepare thy soul by pious readings, prayers, and resolutions, in order that, when the inspiration of grace shall come, thou mayest not receive it in vain.

God will reward thee by conferring

greater grace, by which thou mayest become still stronger, and advance in virtue with greater rapidity.

This is the path which the Saints have followed; if thou follow their examples, thou wilt arrive at their sanctity: for *the arm of the Lord is not shortened.*

Only make a beginning, and thou shalt see the finger of God; deny thyself, and thou shalt taste a hidden manna.

Give thyself over to be borne along by grace, and without much labour thou shalt arrive at the mountain of God to receive a blessing from the Lord.

For they that deliver themselves up liberally to God, *shall renew their strength; they shall take wings, as eagles; they shall fly and not be weary.*

END OF BOOK I.

BOOK II.

CHAPTER I.

That Zeal for Perfection should be fervently sought after from God.

1. *Ask and it shall be given you, seek and you shall find, knock and it shall be opened to you: for every one that asketh, receiveth; and he that seeketh, findeth; and to him that knocks it shall be opened.*

These are the words of our beloved Redeemer, who is far more desirous of giving than we are of receiving, who loves better to be found than we love to seek Him, and who runs to open to us, lest we be kept knocking too long.

9*   113

Behold, with what variety of words He makes known to thee the greatness of His love; see how voluntarily He adds promise to promise, that He may inspire thy prayer with confidence, and prepare thy soul for the reception of His bounty.

2. If then thou wilt be perfect, go to Him, and ask, that it may be given thee, seek that thou mayest find, and knock, that it may be opened to thee.

Or dost thou fear that He will refuse thy petition, fly from thy search, and slight thy knocking?

God is not like men, who become poor by their bounty, because that, which they themselves possess is but little, and received from others: but God is *rich unto all that call upon Him*, and fears not to be impoverished.

Men fear to be dried up like little brooks; but God, who is higher than the Heavens, deeper than hell, and broader than the ocean, however copiously He pours forth the riches of His wisdom and mercy, incurs no loss.

3. Behold, God is ready to give, if only thou be ready to receive.

O infinite condescension of the love of God for us, that He should place at our disposal the riches of His grace!

For what else hath he done? *Ask*, He saith, *and you shall receive;* so that, as it is in our power to ask, it is also in our power to receive whatsoever we demand.

Neither hath He placed any limits to the objects of prayers, so that, if we can but ask it with profit to ourselves, there is nothing whatsoever which we shall not receive.

And if He will bestow upon us whatsoever good things we may ask for, *how much more will He give the Good Spirit to them that ask Him?*

For every best gift and every perfect gift is from above, coming down from the Father of lights.

4. No prayer is more pleasing to God, than one that contains burning desires of perfection, none is more meritorious, none more quickly heard.

The greater and more excellent are the favours we demand of God, the more willingly does He listen to our prayers, for our kind Lord is anxious to heap His graces upon us, and to enrich us.

But he again that asks not for them, or seeks for them carelessly, doth truly a great injury to God.

For the Lord crieth out and saith : *If any man thirst, let him come to Me.* And, *Come to Me, all you that labour and are heavy burdened, and I will refresh you.* And, *Come buy without money;* and many other such words.

And does not he, who though poor and naked, dares nevertheless to disregard such kind words, inflict a great injury on God?

Shall we not say that he, who refuses to ask for the helps unto salvation, which are prepared for him; spurns the gifts of Heaven!

5. O hapless state of blindness in man! Behold the treasures of Heaven are spread out before us, that we may enrich ourselves,

and scarcely will we stretch out our hands to meet our extreme wants.

The fountain of living water is open, the fountain of water springing up to life everlasting, and scarcely ever do we think of slaking our thirst.

We might with ease soar towards Heaven, and yet we prefer to grovel with sinners in the mire of the world.

Is it a small favour that God should satisfy all that beseech His bounty; or would we have Him rain down the treasures of His grace upon those that refuse and despise them?

6. *Let us go therefore with confidence to the throne of grace, that we may obtain mercy:* for great is the abyss of our misery.

Let us beg of God light to see what is well pleasing in His sight, strength to enable us to carry it into execution, fortitude and vigour of mind to persevere.

Behold He Himself wishes to be asked, for He desires to hearken to our prayers, and therefore it is that He commanded his

Apostles, saying: *Pray, that you enter not into temptation.*

And therefore too He admonished all men, saying: *That we ought always to pray and not to faint.*

He that prayeth not when he may do so with ease, is often allowed to fall, that he may see how weak and frail he is, without great help from God.

But he that is humble, and trusteth not in himself, and has recourse to God with confidence in all his wants, understands full well how truly hath the Lord said: *Because he hoped in Me, I will deliver him, I will free him, and I will glorify him.*

Such a one is truly secure under the protection of God, and becomes lord of the treasures of Heaven.

Chapter II.

That little Things are not to be passed over lightly.

1. Son, if thou wilt keep what thou hast, advance in virtue, and be free from many temptations, despise not any good work, however small, and suffer not wilfully any, even the least defect.

The devil is crafty, and especially so when he assails religious; he begins with small things, that by little and little he may come to greater.

Were he at the first onset to assault thee with grievous temptations, being startled on a sudden at the deformity of the sin, thou wouldst curse him, and hurl back his iniquity upon his own head.

But as it is, he takes care to win thee over by a slight temptation, the heinousness of which is but little seen, and hopes to advance later on to more grievous sins.

He has had a long experience, and therefore he dares not look for victory in great matters, if he have not first conquered in things of small, nay, the least importance.

2. As a master is not wont to lead his disciples to higher branches of study, until they have already made sufficient progress in less difficult matters; so also the devil proposes the most grievous temptations only to one that has often yielded to him in trivial faults.

And if he cannot lead him into small faults, he often leaves him in peace, and thinks it in vain to tempt him to grievous sins.

And hence he takes such pains, that thou shouldst abstain from some small good work, and disregard venial faults, and he endeavours to persuade thee not to trouble thyself too much about little things.

3. But if at any time he suggest such thoughts, be on thy guard, lest thou be deceived and give ear to him; for he is the father of lies.

And call to mind rather what I have said to thee: *For I am the way, the truth, and the life.*

I have said before, and I now repeat it: *He that is faithful in that which is least, is faithful also in that which is greater; and he, that is unjust in that which is little, is also unjust in that which is greater*

Meditate on these words and tremble; for what thou neglectest in the beginning, is but little; but what thou disposest thyself to neglect is great, because great things take their rise from small.

Oftentimes from little drops of rain, that fall so noiselessly, rivers become so swollen that they overturn huge buildings. Often too from one small, but unheeded spark of fire, great conflagrations, that cannot be subdued, take their rise.

In like manner, to forget or grow weary of some short prayer, nay some idle conversation, or the avoidance of some little act of self-denial, and any cessation from the pursuit of the least virtue, have finally conducted many into the snares of the devil, and have made them a joy to their enemies.

10

4. Those that fall into great faults, begin with small ones, and no one steals things of value, that was not wont to steal a little often.

So, too, no one proves false to the religious state, which he professed, who has not long before failed in minute observances.

There are many little things that support a man on every side, and if they be removed he must assuredly fall.

Custody of the eyes, and a guard over the other senses, good and spiritual conversation, promptitude in obedience, frequent examination of conscience, avoidance of distractions, mortification of the appetite, restraining thy liberty, and abnegation of thy understanding, keep thee from falling.

Also the external observance of religious discipline, and modesty in the exterior, silence and solitude, submission to poverty, reproofs and the labours of the community, and whatever thy rules prescribe, all greatly assist thee.

5. This it what thou must practise with all diligence, if thou wilt persevere in thy good purpose.

They are small things, it is true, but added together, they are sufficient to defend thy soul and preserve it from evil.

Even as the soldiers, that compose a powerful army, could not, if taken one by one, oppose the enemy; but they carry off the victory, if marshalled together.

I have thus sweetly ordered things, in order that thou mightest not murmur at the difficulty: for I know thy weakness.

Were they great, thou wouldst perhaps excuse thyself on the plea of thy little strength, but they are in truth small, nay, very small, and therefore leave no room for excuse.

Just as Adam had no excuse for eating the apple in the terrestial Paradise, because he might have refrained from it with ease.

6. Wherefore be vigilant, and contemn not small things at any time, but seek to overcome the devil in everything.

However trivial may be the good deed which thou shalt perform, it shall be recompensed with a great reward; but if thou contemn anything, thou shalt quickly see thyself on the brink of ruin.

Amend thy bad habits, *that not a part of a good gift overpass thee;* for so thou shalt acquire great security from the wiles of the devil; and so far from the wicked one leading thee into great peril of thy salvation, thou shalt compel him to occupy himself about the least things; in which, if thou lose, thou art not undone; and if thou gain the victory, he will be put to shame.

CHAPTER III.

That Temptations are useful.

1. LORD, hasten to my aid, for I am daily distressed and almost overwhelmed by many temptations.

Often I am in doubt whether I have resisted them with sufficient firmness, often I feel that I am overcome and cast down.

How long, O Lord, shall this wretched life endure, in which I must fight and resist the devil with such danger of sinning.

Thou knowest, O Lord, how weak and infirm I am.

Arise then and scatter the clouds and tempests, lest I be wholly oppressed and perish.

2. Son, it is not an evil- for temptations and trials to beset thee.

Temptation is burdensome, but it strengthens the soul in patience and fortitude.

Temptation puts thee to confusion now

10*

and then, but it affords thee a great occasion of merit.

Temptation presses hard upon thee, but it is in order that thou mayest acquire greater strength.

Temptation afflicts thee, but that thou mayest justly and usefully suffer something in this life for thy sins.

Temptation seems insupportable to thee, but it is to teach thee to humble thyself, and to fly to Me for refuge.

Temptation vanquishes thee, but only when thou dost trust too much in thyself and thy own strength, and grow torpid in virtue.

3. For the rest, lift up thy voice to Me in temptations, that I may make with temptation issue, and thou mayest be able to bear it.

For though I appear to be far from thee, I am much nearer to thee than thou thinkest.

For I am within thee by My grace, as often as thou dost battle manfully against the temptation; I dwell in thee, I exercise thee, foster thee, stimulate thee, and feel the greatest pleasure at thy resolve to overcome.

And though it be hard for thee to wrestle with the temptation, I know how to render this struggle most pleasing and agreeable to thee.

4. For what can be more pleasing or agreeable to thee, than to know that thou art one of My sheep?

Now, thou mayest hope for this and believe it in perfect assurance, if the devil assail thee with many temptations.

For the devil would have no need of tempting thee, if thou wert of him, or of forcing thee by every vexation to recede from My will, unless he knew for certain that thou dost walk with· Me.

Neither would temptation itself displease thee, unless My love and My grace dwelt in thee.

Wherefore take courage and know, that I have not brought peace, but the sword.

I have often said to thee, and I repeat it:
He that will come after Me, let him deny him-
self, let him take up his cross, and follow Me.

If then thou wilt come after Me into My
glory, take up the cross of temptations
with joy, and fight for thy soul's sake until
victory.

5. If the temptation be grievous, say with
the Hebrew youth : *How can I do this wicked*
thing, and sin against my God?

If the temptation last long, seek some
man appointed by the Superior, take counsel of him, obey him, pour forth thy heart
like water in his sight.

If the temptation be very strong, advance
boldly, pray fervently, labour strenuously,
afflict thy body, humble thy soul before
Me.

Often it is of little avail to fight with the
temptation, but better to turn away one's
eyes from it; for at times, even in battle, it
is safer to fly than to resist.

Some temptations too, that they may not
harm us, should be despised; for, by so

doing, the devil is confounded and loses courage, since he especially detests being held for nothing and despised.

And if sometimes thou dost fall, do not despair, and do not think that all hope of still conquering is taken away.

But rather grieve for thy fall, and persuade thyself that it has happened, either because thou hast been slothful in resisting, or slow to fly, or proud to presume, or unwilling to pray, or because thou hast been negligent in guarding thy heart, or rash in thy judgments, or slothful in fulfilling thy duties.

For, at such times, it is good for thee to be humbled, that thou mayest learn to sympathize with others, and to be more humble in thyself, and to pray more fervently, to undertake the business of thy perfection with greater diligence, and not to trifle with temptation.

CHAPTER IV.

That good Resolutions are to be kept in Time of Desolation.

1. CONSOLATION and spiritual comfort are not always at hand; for God willeth us rather to be tried by patience in desolation and dryness of soul.

Then everything becomes insipid, and what used before to appear to be light and very easy to be done, is wont to become difficult and painful.

And think not, that thou art then abandoned by God, but know that this treatment is dictated by the greatest love for thee, in order that desolation may afford thee no less assistance for acquiring perfection, than celestial consolation itself.

2. See then that thou prove not wanting to thy good purposes; forsake not prayer, neither extinguish the fire of meditation, nor recoil from the path of mortification.

For the devil tempteth thee at such a

time, and, as far as may be, laboureth to persuade thee, that all thy care is to no purpose.

Neither propose to do anything in desolation, for it is then hard to resolve well and wisely, for the mind is drawn aside to vain things, and the heart feeleth itself allured to sensual things.

3. But rather think that consolation was given to thee before, in order that thou mayest now be supported by its fruits.

After autumn, cometh winter; the earth is hardened by frost and beareth no fruit, and still men live not without food, but are nourished by that which they have collected in other seasons.

And so do thou; if void of present consolations, remember the times when celestial visitation filled thee with ineffable sweetness, and do thou now put into execution what thou didst then purpose doing.

If thou didst then write anything good, now open it and read, that the remembrance of past things may serve to alleviate thy present need.   For consolation is useless to thee, if thou strive not to draw such fruit from it for the time of desolation.

4. Think also that God sends thee this trial and tribulation for thy own greater good.

If a guest come to a strange house, the host will give him a light, that he may not trip up and fall in the dark: but when he has learned and often traversed every turn in the house, he trusts to his experience, and cares not for a light.

And so when we entered fresh from the world into religion, and had but an obscure knowledge of spiritual things, God used to lead us by the hand, and enlighten and console us in time of prayer, lest perchance our foot should stumble.

But when we ought to have known well the things that are of the spirit, God leaves us now and then, that we may learn to walk in darkness and aridity, and grow accustomed also to make use of our own industry.

But if we be of good will, this is not a darkness to put us in danger; but we must feel the way with our hands, that we may put in practice what we have been taught by former enlightenment.

He, who in time of desolation shall conduct himself in this manner, shall not only not stumble or fall, but on the contrary shall find an occasion of greater profit and more ample reward.

5. Give therefore to God this proof of thy industry and good will.

For God trieth thee most lovingly, as a mother tries whether her infant can walk; for she retires a little, but does not forsake it, or wholly withdraw herself; and she loveth to be sought and found, and again to take her child to her bosom, and fondle it more lovingly.

And whilst the infant, remembering her former caresses, struggles by every means to bring itself to her bosom, it learns how to use its feet, and strengthens the weakness of its powers by wholesome exercise.

11

Therefore do thou in like manner; and give God thanks for withdrawing Himself a while to thy great profit.

CHAPTER V.

That Common Life is the Means of our Sanctification.

1. LET us give God thanks, who hath in His infinite condescension called us to serve Him under obedience with the best of brethren.

Behold how good and how pleasant it is for brethren to dwell together in unity!

Who can worthily esteem such and so great a boon? Truly we may say of our vocation to religion: *All good things came to me together with her.*

For they, that live in a community of good brethren, are daily stimulated by good example, and inflamed more and more with a desire of their perfection.

No human respect is here to draw us back from virtue; but it rather entices us to it; for the only object of the desires of all, is the perfect attainment of solid virtues.

Thou hast in so many brothers the means of learning humility, simplicity, and fraternal charity.

One will teach thee devotion, another abnegation of the senses, a third, zeal according to knowledge.

From another thou wilt learn prudence of spirit, from another perfect obedience, from another a great affection for poverty; and so of other virtues.

2. O how quickly should we become holy, were we to endeavour to imitate the virtues of others.

Nor should we be less grateful to God for the continual exercise of patience amongst ourselves. For *patience hath a perfect work.*

Now many things happen that constantly afford us the means of so useful an exercise. For either the faults or weaknesses of some of the brethren, or the inconveniences of poverty, or the sharp words of the ill-tempered, or the orders of Superiors, or the burden of others' affairs and occupations, afford us much matter for patience and merit.

And our most benignant God willeth us to be very frequently tried in all these things, that we may quickly learn to go out of ourselves, and be transformed into perfect men.

For he, that has an occasion of self-denial daily offered to him, easily with the grace of God gains all virtues.

3. Then too must be added the vigilance of Superiors and their paternal solicitude for us, and can anything more secure or desirable than this be thought of?

For as the sick have need of more frequent visits from the physician, so it is very good for human weakness to have some one now and then by whom it may be roused.

And as they, that approach a dangerous road, have need to take a guide well acquainted with the way, so it is best for us to obey men that are well versed in virtue.

For we require to be admonished again and again, to be aroused, directed, reprehended, and assisted many times by other offices of charity.

O, would to God that we were not so unmortified, and spurned not the prudence of our spiritual physicians and guides!

Great assuredly would be our security of conscience, great our confidence and consolation.

Let us not then account these things of small value, or murmur at anything, because it goes against the flesh and our passions.

But let us both in word render thanks to God and men, and by our deeds show forth the gratitude of our soul, that all things which happen to us in our religious life may work together for good to us, according to the most benign decree of the Divine Will.

4. There is too a constant practice of pious conversation amongst ourselves; and assuredly the good is not small which is

11*

conferred by those conversations with one another of helping our neighbours, procuring in every way the greatest glory of God, and the easier ways of advancing ourselves by the mortification of defects, and the exercise of virtues.

Times of prayer too, common to all, are fixed, when all with one voice draw down the mercy of God, beseeching Him to be propitious to us and our weakness; thus helping one another, and one compensating by his fervour for the lukewarmness of another.

For the prayer of each one of us is made for the benefit of all; and he, that with good will joins in the prayer of another, carries off no small fruit from this communication, even though perchance he himself be dry in his prayer.

5. See then how profitable to a religious is community life.

By it he is freed from many anxieties, defended from many enemies, provided with most powerful arms, helped on by assistance of all kinds, and disposed in a wonder-ful manner by most holy practices to receive the plentitude of grace.

Woe to him that abuses so many goods to his own perdition, or that yearning for singularities seeks to withdraw himself from the common exercises!

Woe to him, that by torpor, or murmur-ings, or lax opinions, or dissipation, or love of worldly joy, deceives himself, and by the pernicious example of his life becomes the betrayer of his brethren!

Better for him to have remained in the world, than to have become a religious, and to throw obstacles in the way of those that desire to advance.

Let us study, then, to respond worthily to so many and such great favours, lest, perhaps, through our negligence, God re-pent that He has called us into His holy abode, and so let others receive the crown which we have forfeited.

Let us love this life, and seek for no means for our sanctification, that agree not with it.

And since God has pointed out to us this easy path to Heaven, let us not grow slothful, but bear willingly the burdens of our common life, with all alacrity and fervour of spirit, that we may be abundantly comforted by its sweetness and fruits.

Chapter VI.

Of Manifestation of one's Conscience.

1. If thou wilt have much peace of conscience, and be glad in all things, thou shouldst never keep thy temptations, weaknesses, and troubles secret, nor indeed manifest them to every one, but only to thy Superiors, and those that are specially appointed for that purpose.

For as the thorn fixed in the body, must be plucked out for the pain of the body to be allayed, so we must make known our sad thoughts and the suggestions of the devil, if we will have them cease to prick and goad the soul.

Seest thou not, that whoever is oppressed with any grief, is naturally relieved and eased the moment that he exposes the secret wound of his heart? How much more easily will the grace of God and the power of virtue produce the same result?

2. And if thou dost hesitate and defer from day to day to manifest thyself, thou actest imprudently and hatest thyself, since thou refusest so great and so easy a remedy.

If thou wert instantly to overcome thyself and lay open thy conscience, thou wouldst at once allay every agitation of the soul, and live in the greatest tranquillity and security.

For as often as our evils are made known we receive, together with spiritual comfort, an efficacious remedy for them.

If thou hast sinned in anything, or allowed thyself to be somewhat entangled in the snares of the devil, thou mayest easily loose thyself, and restore thyself by the aid of another to thy former state.

But he, that will be his own guide, errs most perilously; for it does not belong to the sick man, but to the physician, to decide about the malady: since it is for this purpose that physicians are employed.

Woe to him that is alone, saith the Scripture, *for when he falleth, he hath none to lift him up.*

However prudent thou mayest be, the devil is still more prudent; and therefore, woe to thee if thou presume to fight against him by thyself.

3. No one can take sufficient precautions for himself, unless he follow the advice of others also; and this is the case not only in spiritual, but also in human affairs.

For often an inordinate love blinds our intellect, and permits it not to see what is most useful.

Often we advise, exhort, and rouse others to virtue, and see clearly and point out what suits them best; but when there is question of ourselves, all at once we become stupid, grow blind, and change our opinion.

Wherefore, though thou canst direct others prudently, leave thyself to be guided by another, lest, perchance, when thou hast preached to others, thou thyself become a reprobate.

4. O how great is the consolation that those religious receive, who, not trusting to themselves, lay themselves open to their Superior, as to a father!

How easily do they find a remedy for their evils, what fortitude in temptation, what preservation from sin!

For the manifestation of one's self is of great efficacy, especially in putting to flight and torturing the devil, who loveth the darkness, that he may safely transform himself into an angel of light.

The devil would wish us never to confess humbly what we have done, or disclose our thoughts to Superiors; but strives to bring us to prefer being led by our own judgment and opinion, in order that we may not learn from veteran warriors, how to vanquish and confound him.

If the counsels of the devil remain not concealed, he himself cannot endure the light, but flies away destitute of hope.

There is nothing that more quickly takes away his courage, and makes him grow faint hearted, than that his stratagems be known.

5. Often too he ceases to tempt, if one is wont to disclose the temptation; for he is fully aware that he will be vanquished and daily become weaker.

Whatever evil he may suggest, whatever disturbance he may create, whatever trouble he may cause, he is forced to despair of victory, unless he can inflict a secret wound.

For humility is a great virtue, by which the secret places of the conscience are laid open; and the devil has no power over the truly humble.

Simplicity is a great virtue, by which the heart is poured out like water before the vicars of God, and is superior to all worldly cunning.

It is great prudence to mistrust ourselves,

and to receive all the blows of the devil upon the buckler of another.

An humble manifestation of ourselves, a good will to make progress, and simple obedience have great merit.

Great is the strength of him that has a defender: *For a brother, that is helped by a brother, is as a strong city.*

For the grace of God strengthens the humble and the simple, and God hath chosen the foolish things of the world to confound the strength of the devil.

CHAPTER VII.

That in the Way of Perfection we must proceed with Order and by Detail.

1. SON, there are very many things that keep thee back from the desired perfection of virtues.

Some darken the understanding, others weaken the will, others again lead to drow-

12

siness and inaction, through the contagious influence of the senses of the body.

See what is thy state; thy obstacles are the tongue, the eyes, the ears, and the concupiscence of the members.

Thy obstacles are the liberty and wanderings of the imagination, love of ease, curiosity to see the things of the world, ignorance of spiritual things, and prejudicial opinions.

Thy obstacles are thy past sins, by which thy soul feels itself weakened, and bad habits which thou hast not yet mortified.

Thy obstacles are love and fear of the world, inordinate meddling in business and cares about vain things.

2. But let not the multitude of thy enemies fill thee with dread. Neither attack them all together, nor presume on a speedy conquest. Divide them, and then thou wilt rule.

O if thou didst understand what I mean, and understanding it wouldst put it into execution! it would be an easy and certain, yea, even a pleasant and compendious way to arrive at perfection.

He, that would overcome all his defects at once, laboureth much, but scarce gains anything.

The mind is wearied by importunity, and in a short time is rendered useless for the fight, and filled with confusion.

The will too becomes weaker by such combats, and because the fruit of amendment seems but little, it is easy to lose heart and draw back from the strife.

3. And hence, when the devil sees any one fervent in spirit, and cannot draw him back by any other way from the service of God, he takes care to make him wage war against all his vices with disorderly and imprudent haste.

The devil, believe Me, feels no alarm whenever he hears any one say: *Now I wish to be reformed in everything, and to become a Saint:* but rather smiles, for he knows that he has by his craft deceived many that made such resolutions.

But his greatest fear is whenever he perceives a fervent religious applying every engine against some one principal vice, and labouring with energy and alacrity for one victory only.

For the latter having taken on him a labour equal to his strength, will be able to labour constantly, and having gained one victory, however slight it may be, to advance to greater ones in security.

But he that in the ardour of his zeal proposed too much, though he begin with courage, still may be safely presumed to be about to fail through the weakness of his nature.

4. Wherefore consider thyself and thy defects: select amongst thy vices what thou shouldst first assail, what next.

Advance from those that are more easily vanquished, to more difficult things, or even begin by cutting out the very root of thy vices, that thou mayest cut down the rest in a summary manner.

And say not: *Henceforth I will not be*

proud, I will not be angry, I will not be lazy.
This is also too much.

But if thou hast made up thy mind to fight against pride, have a care, in the first place, to be silent about thyself; next, if any little humiliation befall thee, not to murmur at it; then, to seek from time to time to be humiliated; and so on.

In 'this manner vices are easily rooted out; for the labour is divided, so that the strength of the soul is not impaired, and its constancy prevented.

Thus too, he that would bring down a worthless tree, does not attempt it by one violent effort, nor think to cut it down with one blow, but gradually cuts each root with many blows.

5. If thou labour at thy amendment after this manner, thou wilt quickly acquire perfection.

And though thou hast to fight a long time against a single vice, fear not; having slain the leader, the rest of thy enemies will

12*

fly ; and having overturned the column the rest of the house will fall.

For vices, like virtues, are naturally linked together, and one cannot be conquered without weakening and injuring the others.

Therefore having destroyed one vice, the rest will grow languid, and victory over them will very easily ensue.

CHAPTER VIII.

That the Meditation of Heavenly Things is necessary.

1. SON, so long as thou dost live on earth, thou art liable to many errors and evil affections ; and here thou art both inconstant in good purposes, and often departest from the right path.

Do thou then, that art ever infirm, receive spiritual medicines with pleasure, and be solicitous about a frequent use of them.

If thou contemn them, thou wilt not

only at once fall short of perfection, but be in peril of the salvation of thy soul hereafter.

Now of these remedies some are not fit for all times, but are to be used with discretion, and not employed without prudent advice; but some may be used to advantage every day, and repeated oftentimes the same day.

2. Let thy daily medicine be the meditation of heavenly things, to enlighten the mind with Divine light, and recall the will from inordinate desires.

The meditation of the eternal truths, of the examples of Christ and the Saints, is a great good; it is, I say, a great good, and the beginning of every good.

Meditation is the workshop of the spirit, the auxiliary of virtues, and the nursery of good works.

Meditation does away with prejudices, suggests useful things, destroys concupiscence, and rends asunder the nets of the devil.

Meditation is the mother of true and solid devotion; for it leads the will courageously and sweetly, to perform that which is pleasing in the sight of God.

3. Scarcely any devotion is true, if meditation has not preceded it, for it cannot be lasting, since it has not a foundation in the solid preparation of the understanding.

Such a devotion is fickle and inconstant, and is found wanting, when temptation or aridity arises.

Look at seculars that do not practice meditation; how few live well; how many follow the way of perdition; how many do not even think of God, or eternal life!

For *with desolation*, He saith, *is the whole earth made desolate, because there is no one that thinketh in his heart.*

And even if some of them live well and are lovers of virtue, how often do they fluctuate, or even fall into sins, unless they think frequently of the eternal things.

To-day, they are devout; to-morrow, they are sluggish in the Divine service; and so all their life they build up and destroy by turns; and never finish their spiritual edifice.

4. Meditation is the sweet repose and recreation of the spiritual man, no less necessary for the soul, than daily food or sleep for the body.

Meditation is the mirror of the soul, in which it should behold itself every day, until it purge itself from all foulness, and array itself in every grace in order to please Christ.

Meditation is the noblest exercise of self-denial, the torch of the mind, the life of the will, the bearer of Divine grace, the anticipated likeness and imitation of the joys of Heaven. Never, therefore, must we be sluggish in so holy an exercise, but even if the devil strives to produce a loathing for it and bring on distractions of mind, we must labour with all assiduity, and persevere with alacrity.

5. If at morn thou rise with the Prophet and laying aside all other cares, meditate

on the words of the Lord attentively, the whole day will now be easily sanctified.

Mortification will be sweet, solitude amiable, silence agreeable, and devotion familiar.

The endurance of community life will become easy, the mind patient in labours, and thy zeal ardent in procuring the glory of God.

The rigour of poverty will not displease thee, nor the load of humiliations oppress thee, nor the weight of other grievances, nor the assault of persecutions disturb thee.

If thou meditate devoutly, thou wilt find thyself prepared to endure all these things, yea, thou wilt even long for them with the greatest ardour, in imitation of Christ.

For meditation teaches, how good it is to deny our evil desires, and exercise patience, and it adds the sharpest goads to the will, that it cease not running.

6. But if thou be little solicitous about holy meditation, and either altogether abandon it, or perform it by routine, think not that thou wilt live that day like a religious.

For compunction will not please, nor self-denial, nor silence, nor any exercise of virtue.

A little labour will easily oppress thee, the necessity of obeying will sadden thee, every burden will seem insupportable.

It is not only once that thou hast experienced this; for never hast thou lived more distracted, and less religiously, than when thou hast neglected the practice of meditation.

Learn then from the inspection of thy own life, how much need thou hast of meditation, and whatever happen that is new, or great, or unexpected, allow not thyself to be ever impeded in so holy an exercise.

Chapter IX.

That the Conscience must be frequently examined.

1. PLACE thyself often in the presence of God, and laying aside all superfluous cares diligently examine thy works.

Let thy first care be to know intimately and to endeavour to amend thyself; lest perchance the Jebusite grow up in secret and gain strength against thee.

The soul is like a garden; it should be cleared every day from the evil growth of concupiscence.

We should apply ourselves daily to the cultivation of virtues, and consider what progress we have, or should have made.

Our good resolutions are to be daily renewed and confirmed, that the will may not languish and grow cold.

All this is necessary for him, that would make progress, and because we have not yet wholly renounced our vices, we must take care to put off each day some portion of the old man.

2. This is the way along which all the Saints proceeded, and after having repressed in a short time all their evil inclinations, raised themselves to the pinnacle of virtue.

O what purity of conscience did the Fathers that served God in the desert, reach, and how many thousands of monks did they happily lead to perfection!

But the practice of examining their life was familiar to them, and by daily and continued search into themselves they put into instant execution the things that by nightly contemplation they had learned to do.

And hence the custom of examination of conscience has been introduced into all religious orders by their holy founders.

For by this inquiry a man knows his bad habits and inclinations better, is confounded and sorry for his faults, resolves on their amendment with great efficacy, determines to punish himself if he fall wil-

13

fully, and often invokes the assistance of God; and by so doing, he represses vices and gains much good.

3. But a much greater and more frequent necessity of self-inspection is incumbent on all those who have to procure the salvation of their neighbour.

Many would pass for good religious, had they only to attend to themselves in some solitude; but because far greater virtue is requisite for apostolical men, they do not appear with safety to themselves amongst worldlings.

He that hath not laid solid foundations of virtue, mixes with peril in the ministries of an active life.

The mind of the imperfect man is easily distracted in the midst of business, and so absorbed, that frequently he forgets himself, whilst providing for others.

And since we are all imperfect, we should frequently look into ourselves and demand before God, an account of all our works.

Thus it will be easy to correct forthwith

what verges towards evil, and close up every entrance to the devil.

Thus too what conduces to the salvation of others will be more perfectly and prudently performed; since all will be able to see more easily and weigh more attentively the conditions of the things to be done.

4. If any one would be very useful to his neighbour, he should search out all the avenues of the human heart, he should know the snares of the devil, the cunning of the passions, the infirmities of human nature and their remedies, the multiplied ways of Divine inspirations, and be perfectly skilled in the entire art of spiritual warfare.

But all this is learned by one's own experience and consideration, rather than by the reading of ascetical books.

Hence the Scripture saith: *What doth he know, that hath not been tried?*

But he that seldom and hastily examines himself, perceives not these conflicts of nature and grace within himself, and neither detects the crafty subterfuges of the passions, nor can he know the most useful and expeditious remedies for spiritual diseases.

Therefore, do we see that some ignorant, but spiritual men, render far more service to their neighbours, than others that are learned and instructed, but less solicitous about themselves.

5. Keep this well in mind; no progress in perfection can be hoped for, no assistance to our neighbour will be of any efficacy, except by the power of the grace of God.

· Now God is accustomed to distribute His gifts so much the more liberally, as He sees one more diligent in purifying his conscience.

Therefore exercise thyself in searching and persecuting thy vices; think how thou mayest daily, either more fully mortify some passion, or rear up some tender virtues with greater care, or discover some better mode of action in all thy affairs.

From this thou wilt gain great purity of conscience, great experience and prudence, and great tranquility and comfort.

The grace of God will abound in thee, temptations will be lessened, and the whole spiritual edifice, resting on a firm foundation, will rise to its destined height.

Thus too thou wilt grow accustomed to stand before the Lord with familiarity, to raise thy mind oftener to heavenly things, to direct thy intention to God in due order, and from the most trivial actions to gain a great reward of merit.

Chapter X.

That Devotion to the Saints is most useful for those
that desire to advance in Perfection.

1. TRULY *the children of this world are
wiser in their generation, than the children of
light.*

For seculars, when they cannot by themselves obtain all the earthly good they
desire, court the rich and noble, and most
cunningly endeavour to turn their power
to their own advantage.

But we, though spiritually destitute and
poor, live almost in total forgetfulness of
the Saints, by whose prayers we might
obtain many great favours.

Seculars, though oftentimes repelled by
the powerful, return, ask, beseech with
tears; but we, though we shall be most
kindly received, are not aroused from our
inaction.

They are very pressing in their petitions,
wait a long time, and use every means to

carry off by their importunity some of the favours which they stand in need of; but we, even to obtain favours from on high, scarce ever have a devout word to utter.

2. O shame on us! Is it because God is the Supreme Author and Dispenser of all good things, that the Saints are to be neglected, or their invocations deemed of little avail?

Seek not excuses for thy sloth; the Saints are most dear to God, and if they ask for anything, they obtain it much more quickly and easily.

God Himself has often decreed to bestow His favours by the hands of His Saints, that He may honour them the more, and teach us also to honour and reverence them.

And therefore did Christ call His Apostles not servants, but friends; and the Prophet saith: *Thy friends, O God, are made exceedingly honourable, their principality is exceedingly strengthened.*

3. This then is the will of God, that we

obtain very many blessings through the Saints that are in Heaven.

Does it seem to thee a little thing to use the patronage of those that have been in this very same life, and in the same dangers?

They too have suffered very many things, and therefore easily have compassion on us.

Or is it a small thing to be able to make the friends of Christ and the sharers in His Kingdom thy friends?

Resolve then to serve them; see how thou mayest become dearer to them; and thus thou shalt have freer access to God.

As their feasts draw nigh, purify thy conscience with greater diligence, that thou mayest be more worthy of their protection.

Read their lives; and ponder deeply the way in which they became holy, in order to keep to the same path.

Devotion to the Saints consists in great part in endeavouring with the grace of God to rival their merits; and it is for this very reason that the Church also commands, that the Saints be frequently honoured and praised.

4. Choose then some of the Saints for special patrons and masters in virtue; study to become pleasing to them by resemblance of life.

Let it be the first and principal tribute of thy devotion towards them, to desire to be like them; then, to beseech them to obtain suitable aid from God.

Ask of one to imitate his patience, another his humility, and a third his compunction and charity.

' But meanwhile attend to thyself, and join fasting and other mortifications to thy prayers, for so they will be more efficacious in obtaining.

5. But let thy special care be to honour the Blessed Virgin and Mother of God; for the mother by herself has more power than all friends and servants.

For the Mother of our Redeemer loves us more ardently, since she far excels all the Saints in charity.

This most Blessed Virgin asks like a queen from a king; as mistress, she provides; and as mother, she dispenses the treasures of Heaven.

It is also of great merit with Christ to love and honour His Mother exceedingly; for Christ Himself also loves and honours her most of all.

They, that take Mary for their mother, are truly considered and protected by Christ as His Brethren.

Let us then seek to please her above all others, and let us not rest satisfied until we feel that she loves us most ardently.

Nor are monthly tributes of honour sufficient; she must be honoured with daily prayers and works: for children need their mother's aid each day, and oftentimes in the day.

They, that are wont to serve the Mother of God in sincerity and devotion, feel great help in temptations, solace in tribulations, strength in labours, protection in dangers, sweetness in the spiritual life, security in death, and eternal happiness in Heaven.

Chapter XI.

That we should frequently apply ourselves to reading
Spiritual Books.

1. He that desires not to grow faint in
the way of virtue, should each day take
some spiritual food, and thus preserve his
strength.

And since the mind of man is unstable
in the consideration of heavenly things, and
is easily distracted on every occasion by
sensible things, to read and ponder well
pious books is most useful.

By this means the importunate assaults
of troublesome imaginations are more easily
kept away, and the soul is peacefully and
sweetly enriched.

It is easier also to follow the guidance of
others, and to use an instruction already
prepared, than to open a way for one's self.

2. Thou wilt there find many incentives
and aids to virtue, which thou hast not yet
known or considered.

Whatever pious and holy men have by long contemplations and tears deserved to be taught by God, thou wilt make thy own with little labour, if only thou desire it.

The experience of others will aid thy inexperience, their fervour thy tepidity, their devotion thy dryness, their wisdom thy ignorance.

If thou couldst speak face to face with those Saints, thou wouldst leave all to be with them; behold thou mayest now enjoy their conversation familiarly as much as thou wilt.

Moreover, to read their writings is often more useful than even to converse with them; for what thou hast read once thou mayest at will read again many times, and meditate on with great attention, until thou hast thoroughly learnt it; and when it has escaped thy memory, thou canst again recall it to mind.

3. The whole life of a true religious, should be nothing else but to search out the will of God in all things, and having found it to put it into execution.

Be not then negligent in reading spiritual books; for if thou wilt open the hearing of thy soul, thou wilt hear the voice of God proceeding from them.

It is assuredly a great gift of God, that He should mercifully vouchsafe to speak to us by books, often too when we are distracted and turning a deaf ear to the internal whispering of His grace.

For we hear the voice of God more easily when reading, than when thinking with the mind alone, and hence also good reading is wont to be the teacher of good thoughts.

For we must always, since such is the bent of our nature, be thinking of something; but to prescribe the subjects of our thoughts belongs much less to nature than to each one's own voluntary preparation and election.

If thou leave alone a wild olive tree, it remains a useless tree; but if thou ingraft a good olive, it will bear much fruit.

If therefore thou wilt prevent evil thoughts and ingraft good ones, give thy

14

soul spiritual food, that it may not, by want of it, be turned to sensible objects.

Thus wilt thou easily preserve recollection of mind throughout the day, and in all thy occupations be present to God.

4. Have then a fixed time for applying daily to so useful an exercise; and unless some serious obstacle impede thee, never omit it.

Many sinners have with the grace of God been converted by pious reading; many holy men also have by the same means reached a more holy life.

And as perverse and dishonest reading cannot but cause serious injury, so from spiritual books many wonderful good things must proceed.

For as immoral reading causes first bad thoughts and desires, then bad words and works, to the scandal and ruin of many, so pious reading brings forth holy thoughts and holy desires, and not so long after there will follow in its train holy deeds too and a holy conversation to the glory of God, and the great edification of men.

Chapter XII.

That to love Silence is necessary for him that desires to make Progress.

1. NOTHING distracts and impedes the mind from the pursuit of virtue more than an immortified habit of talking.

A man full of tongue, saith the Holy Scripture, *shall not be established on the earth.* And elsewhere: *In the multitude of words there shall not want sin;* and, *He that useth many words shall hurt his own soul.*

For he that speaks much cannot weigh well what he is going to say, and how he should speak, or whether he should speak at all.

Nor can he look to himself, on account of his continual distraction of mind; but whilst he is occupied with useless things and unmindful of his own danger, he is taken in the snare of the devil.

As a city that lieth open, and is not encompassed with walls, so is a man that cannot refrain his own spirit in speaking. .

2. Be not then deceived; so long as thou hast not learned to refrain thy tongue, thou wilt not advance.

Therefore, the Prophet prayeth: *Set a watch, O Lord, before my mouth, and a door round about my lips.*

Recollect thy past life and tell me; whenever thou hast spent the entire day in hearing and relating the deeds of others, what spiritual profit hast thou made?

Perhaps thou wilt find no day fuller of sins than that on which thou didst abandon all care for thyself, and give free reins to thy loquacity.

Thou hast uttered many words, but thou hast scattered the spirit of devotion to the winds.

Thou hast sought after ridiculous tales, and choked up the remembrance of the eternal truths.

Thou hast thought of many vain and useless things, and forgotten what should have been most necessary for thee.

Listen then to St. James: *If any man*

think himself to be religious, not bridling his tongue, but deceiving his own heart, this man's religion is vain.

Know too, moreover, that *every idle word that men shall speak, they shall render an account for it in the day of judgment.*

Of this Christ Himself, who will be thy judge hereafter, has admonished thee.

8. O what facility for advancing wouldst thou find, if thou wert to abstain from superfluous conversations!

Mightest thou not labour all that time with profit in procuring the amendment of thy vices?

Many things remain for thee to learn, either from the science of the saints or from human teaching; all this thou mightest easily learn, if thou wouldst be silent.

Thou couldst write more for the edification and salvation of thy neighbour, exercise more works of charity, snatch more prey from the devil.

But if it grieve thee to be silent and remain in thy cell, thou wilt lose all this,

· 14*

and bring trouble and loss on thy brethren.

4. Learn then what thou oughtest to do; it is not without grave reasons that the law of silence has been placed in the rules of monasteries by their holy founders.

A habit of silence makes us avoid many occasions of sinning, and makes us forget the bad habit of speaking from impetuosity and passion.

A habit of silence gives great opportunities of listening to others, and learning how it is necessary to speak in a religious manner.

A habit of silence disposes the soul to hearken to the secret whisperings of God, and converse sweetly with the Lord, for He saith: *I will lead her into the wilderness, and I will speak to her heart.*

A habit of silence frees us from many anxieties and vanities, and begets great peace.

5. Remember that admirable saying: *If any one offend not in word, the same is a perfect man.*

See what an easy path to perfection the Holy Scriptures point out to those that will.

It is not placed beyond the sea, that thou shouldst say : who will go thither? nor in the clouds, that thou shouldst say : who will ascend to Heaven? nor beyond the limits of thy power.

It is near unto thee, it is before thee, it is within thee, according to the word of the Lord : *The kingdom of Heaven is within you.*

Bridle therefore thy tongue, and thou shalt quickly overcome thy other vices, and acquire perfection.

It is difficult not to fall whilst speaking; and therefore resolve to be silent as much as thou canst.

CHAPTER XIII.

That exterior Modesty is necessary for a Religious.

1. PERFECTION is a thing of the interior, and has its dwelling in the soul; but do not therefore think, that all care for the external regulation of the movements of the body is to be thrown away.

The whole man came from God in the beginning; and therefore, the whole man should be directed so as to serve God internally and externally, at the same time.

The whole man will reap the reward of his merits in Heaven; therefore, the whole man should be well ordered in this life.

Permit not anything to be in thee that may offend the eye of any one; but moderate all thy movements in the manner that is beseeming a lover of holiness.

Picture to thyself Christ our Lord as present before thee, and learn from Him exterior gravity; also patience, humility and all modesty.

2. *When a strong man armed keepeth his court, those things are in peace, which He possesseth.*

If therefore thou wilt preserve peace of heart, keep the court of thy heart, that is, the external senses.

Think not that thy soul can be well ordered within, if external order be despised.

The soul to the body, and the body to the soul cling to each other mutually, and form one whole in such a manner, that in action they naturally respond to each other.

He, that knoweth not how to rule over the senses of his body, will still less be able to curb his interior passions.

For he that cannot turn away his eyes from unlawful or curious things, can hardly avert his thoughts from the same, and preserve himself from bad desires.

3. If thou wilt give thy attention to God, give no opening to created things, but close thy senses to them that they enter not; for if they enter in, thou wilt hardly cast them out, to give place to God.

Yesterday, thou didst seek after and behold many things; and to-day, thou canst not calm down their impressions, and check thy imagination.

Another evil also arises; for the soul in a manner goeth out by the senses and loseth its strength.

As good liquor loses its spirit when the covering of the vessel is taken away, and little by little grows sour, so the soul that is not guarded in the exterior, suffers the spirit of devotion to evaporate, and begins little by little to displease God.

And as the vessel is filled with dust and dirt, when the covering is taken off, so too the soul is stained, as soon as the custody of the senses is taken away.

4. It is no small victory to know practically how to become perfect; the whole power of the soul is necessary for it.

See then that thou weaken not thyself; for he, that despises exterior modesty, draws on himself many cares, and having increased the number of his enemies divides his forces against each, and thus is much reduced in strength.

Make a strong citadel for thy soul within the barriers of which it may fight in safety; close the gates of thy senses, and open them not to thy enemies, but only to bring in with circumspection some spiritual provisions.

Consider what men do when any grave business is urgent upon them; they separate themselves from others, and having closed their chamber discuss the means of freeing themselves from it.

Do thou also act in a similar manner; thou hast a difficult business in hand; and closed and barred within thyself, see how thou mayest correct thyself; for otherwise, thou wilt not be able.

5. He that guards himself from the wandering of his senses, although he may have often to be engaged with men, receives no harm; for he goes like a captain surrounded by his soldiers.

Rather he does hurt to the devil, for he

invites men to a good life by the example of his modesty.

Exterior modesty is most worthy of admiration in the eyes of men; and he that composes modestly his eyes, voice and every gesture, appears like an Angel in the midst of men.

Such a man is willingly listened to and easily persuades; for he seems to be one come down from Heaven, and speaking in the name of God.

And even though his tongue be silent, he preaches by example, which is often of greater efficacy; as indeed we read that the blessed Francis once preached.

But if we are disordered and discomposed in our external movements, not only we shall not persuade others, but we shall become objects of ridicule, and justly to be reproved.

For the seriousness of our ministry agrees not with lightness of carriage, nor the religious dress with disorderly habits.

6. See, however, that thou be not solicit-

ous about exterior modesty only, and neglect that which is interior.

Let thy principal care be of internal cleanness and order: *With all watchfulness keep thy heart, because life issueth out from it.*

If the root groweth dry, the tree perisheth ; and if modesty flow not from the heart, it lasteth not.

As external disorder disorders the soul also, so too the disorder of the soul is manifested by the movements of the body. And therefore the Scripture saith: *A man is known by his look; and a wise man, when thou meetest him, is known by his countenance.*

And elsewhere it saith: *As the faces of them that look therein, shine in the water, so the hearts of men are laid open to the wise.*

The shadow follows the body, and the external demeanour of the body the internal affections of the soul. We must therefore put in order our internal affections, in order that external modesty may be habitually maintained.

15

Chapter XIV.

That it behooves us to acquire an intimate Knowledge
of Christ.

1. *This is eternal life, that they know Thee,
the only true God, and Jesus Christ, whom
thou hast sent.*

Blessed is he that studies daily to know
Christ more perfectly, and advance in His
love!

The knowledge of Christ is more perfect
than all other knowledge, and beyond all
makes the soul grow rich.

The knowledge of Christ pours joy and
sweetness into the soul, and renders the
exercise of all virtues most easy.

O, would to God, that we applied ourselves with as much diligence to gain an
intimate knowledge of Christ, as we care
to learn human sciences and the vainest
things.

Christ, our Lord, is a great and choice
book; he, that knoweth how to read and

understand it, will very soon acquire all wisdom.

2. Christ is the way, the truth, and the life; if any one enter by Him, he will be saved.

Through Jesus are we associated and in a manner ingrafted into the Divine Nature; through Him we have received the adoption of children of God, and the right of inheritance.

Without Christ, we are darkness, we can do nothing, we have nothing; unless we study to please Him, to please all men will profit us nothing.

Therefore, we must, with all solicitude, search out the intimate sentiments of His heart, that His sentiments and desires may also be our sentiments and desires.

Love not, or esteem as great, anything that thou hast not seen Christ esteem and love.

3. Now what Christ thinks and desires, thou wilt easily find out from His life and teaching.

For the law of Christ declareth that blessed are the poor in spirit, blessed are the meek, blessed are they that hunger and thirst after justice, blessed are they that mourn, blessed are the clean of heart, blessed are' the merciful, and blessed are those that suffer persecution for justice sake.

All these things did Christ value highly and love above all others, so that He even chose them for Himself.

Meditate therefore on them one by one, such as Christ hath vouchsafed to show them forth in Himself for our example, and thou wilt quickly arrive at an intimate knowledge of Christ.

In like manner, Christ came to cast fire on the earth, to seek His Father's, and not His own glory, to expel the inordinate love of creatures, to teach the simplicity of the dove, the prudence of the serpent, a child-like ingenuousness and humility, and many other things that have been handed down to us by the Evangelists.

Consider then each thing well, and thou wilt understand in what things Christ took complacency.

If thou once penetrate the excellence and holiness of this doctrine, thou wilt find all the treasures of the wisdom and knowledge of God hidden in Christ; and thou wilt be enriched as much as thou canst receive.

4. He that loves ardently never forgets his beloved, but attends to all his words, and admires and esteems all his actions.

Thus, then, it is fitting that the lovers of Christ dwell on His words and works, that they may know Him more intimately, and even love Him more perfectly.

Consider how long Christ lived in humility for thy sake, what love He has ever shown us, what patience, mercy and sweetness.

Whatever favours He is said to have granted others, think that He has also bestowed on thee; for they are often common to all, and thou perhaps hast received much more than others.

15*

Whatever He hath suffered for all, believe that He hath suffered specially for thee, and say with the Apostle: *Who hath loved me and delivered Himself for me.*

5. O how great a condescension, that the Only Begotten of God should for my sake come down from Heaven, for my sake weep in a manger, for my sake hunger and thirst, for my sake be straightened by tribulations, for my sake be scourged, wounded, scoffed at and slain !

O would that we employed ourselves willingly in the contemplation of these mysteries! Would that we remembered, that He hath done all this, to teach us what we must do to please Him.

Consider too, with what favours He hath enriched thee in spite of thy demerits, and what he hath promised to give.

Thou wilt then more thoroughly recognize the bowels of His mercy, and be moved to thanksgiving for them.

For though all things are in Him, and / by Him, still thou hast received, and art yet to receive all spiritual blessings in a special manner through Christ.

From Him, is remission of sins and the infusion of the Holy Spirit; from Him, the source of all graces and all merits; from Him, the spiritual life of the soul in this world, and its eternal glory in the life to come.

If thou ask for anything, thou wilt not obtain it in any other name, but that of Jesus Christ; for no other name is given to us by which we may be saved.

Whatever danger or tribulation assails thee, it is only by Him that thou wilt overcome it, as it is only by Him that thou hast until now been the victor. Thou shouldst then care for nothing else in this world, but to become daily more dear to Christ.

6. Jesus Christ loves thee beyond what words can say, and were it necessary for Him to die for thee again, He would again and again do so with the greatest joy.

Neglect not, I pray thee, by these or similar reasons, to acquire a knowledge of Christ, the most intimate thou canst.

Thou wilt see how sweetly such a knowledge will draw thee to a perfect imitation of Him.

Turn over His life in thy mind during the day, and daily meditate on something of His doctrine; thus wilt thou be able to conform thy judgment to His unerring judgment.

Examine with what affection He has executed His Father's will, even unto the death of the cross; with what gladness He emptied Himself, to make thee great in His kingdom.

Reflect how hard and thorny were the paths He traversed to snatch thee, His lost sheep from wolves, and conduct thee back to His fold in the most tender manner.

Admire in everything *the riches of His bounty*, and weigh deeply what is just for thee to return Him for so much condescension.

7. He is truly unworthy of the love of Christ, who neglects to foster a love for Christ by such aids.

He is unworthy of Christ who studies not to know Christ well; *for I know My sheep,* He saith, *and My sheep know Me.*

Nor can he be a good soldier of Christ, who does not study to know his own Captain, and knows not what pleases Him.

Hearken then to the precept of the Apostle : *Put you on the armour of God, to wit, Christ, that you may be able to stand against the deceits of the devil.*

It is an inestimable good, though we be ignorant of every thing else, to know Christ intimately and love Him alone.

And it is an inestimable gain, abandoning everything else, to take up our abode in His sacred wounds.

Chapter XV.

That Reproofs are to be willingly hearkened to.

1. If any one say that he has no sin, the truth is not in him, for *we all offend in many things.*

And therefore, it was said by a certain one: *No one is born without vices, he is the best who has the fewest.*

All our endeavours then should be directed to not despising their remedies, since we are involved in many defects.

Thou shouldst in truth ask thy brothers not to be loath to admonish thee, if they perceive anything in thee that is faulty.

And thou shouldst consider them so much the more friendly to thee, as they more frequently lay open to thee thy faults.

And thou shouldst be still more anxious for this to be done by Superiors, since thy Superiors are to thee in place, not only of friends, but also of parents, and are bound to look to thy perfection.

2. *He that hateth reproof is foolish*, proud, perverse, a land of reprobation and well nigh cursed.

For he that hateth reproof loveth sin.

If indeed it displease thee to be still imperfect, complain not at the reprehensions of thy elders and equals; yea, suffer thyself to be admonished even by inferiors.

And if any one chide thee, listen to his reproof with thanksgiving, and strive to amend.

To reprehend one in fault is a hard office, and all have not sufficient courage for it.

Though perchance thou wilt find many that blush not to accuse others from petulance and temerity; but few, and very few, know how to do it with charity.

Therefore, be persuaded that there is no one that loves thee more than he that fears not to wrestle against thy vices.

3. *Open rebuke is better than hidden love*, saith the Scripture. *And better are the*

wounds of a friend, than the deceitful kisses of an enemy.

Therefore, he that rebukes and reprehends thee, is more useful to thee than all that praise and flatter thee.

As much as they, that without thy hearing murmur of thee, do thee more harm, so much the more do they assist thee, that in thy hearing only disclose to thee thy defects.

Thou shouldst then be most friendly to him that admonishes thee more freely.

But if any one, especially a Superior, seeing thee full of defects, is silent and dares not reprove thee, go to him, and with all modesty persuade him not to do thee this injury.

For oftentimes he abstains from rebuke, because he sees thee not sufficiently disposed to hear it.

Confess, therefore, thy infirmity to him, and promise that thou wilt henceforward hold his admonition in great esteem.

For if thou give him occasion to judge

otherwise of thee, thou wilt be abandoned to thyself, like one labouring under an incurable disease, according to the Holy Scripture: *Rebuke not a scorner, lest he hate thee.*

4. Think that thou art sick, woe to thee if thou compel the physicians to be silent and depart from thee.

Thou wilt neither apply an useful remedy to thyself, nor allow it to be applied by others.

If any one dare to touch thee, unless thou art patient, everything will be filled with complaints and wranglings.

O how much evil may thy pride and impatience and bitterness do thee, if they induce others to keep silence!

O how much better would it be for thee, to thank with true humility all that admonish thee!

How much more easily would others exercise this office of fraternal correction in thy regard, if they did not fear to give thee some occasion of resisting them.

16

Learn then, although thou mayest think that thou hast not erred, to hear a reproof with all humility; thus thou wilt be able to know and overcome thy defects.

END OF BOOK II.

BOOK III.

CHAPTER I.

Of Religious Poverty.

1. *If thou wilt be perfect, go sell what thou hast and give to the poor, and come, follow Me.*

These are the words by which the Lord Jesus admonished a certain young man, who was thinking of a perfect life.

But he went away sad, for he was very rich, and because he was not truly desirous of being perfect, he had not strength of mind to put into execution the counsel of the Lord.

We too are equally deceived, if we desire to retain anything in religion, or long for

195

any of the things we have already left behind in the world.

2. We quitted the world, that we might
serve Christ, and by good deeds deserve to ·
be translated into His glory.

But how can we be the servants of
Christ, if our heart repose in creatures, and
far from Christ?

However little and mean may be the
object, which gains our affection, it deprives
us of the greatest good, that is, the desire of
perfection and holiness of life.

3. Thou hast seen no one advance in
perfection, that has not made the most
vigorous efforts to wean his heart wholly
from all created things;

No one soaring to the heights of the
Holy Mountain, that has not withdrawn
his feet from the mire of sensible objects;

No one approaching the Holy City of
God, that has not considered himself a pil-
grim upon earth, and bid a final adieu to
everything around him, that he might run
with Christ in greater freedom.

4. Created things clog the soul, and are an obstacle to the following of Christ.

Therefore hath Christ said, that it is easier for a camel to pass through the eye of a needle, than for a rich man to enter the gate of the kingdom of Heaven. For it is hard to abound in riches, and not to love delicacies.

And hence did the Prophet wisely admonish us: *If riches abound set not thy heart upon them.* And we should rejoice to renounce everything, that we may prove to Almighty God, that we love and esteem Him above all riches and pleasures.

5. Truly we are blessed, that have voluntarily and sincerely left all things with Peter, and followed after Jesus, bearing our cross.

Nor do we fear the threats which Christ hath uttered against the rich; but on the contrary, we look forward to a reward in the regeneration: provided, we preserve ourselves perfectly in holy poverty.

But if we return imprudently to any of
16*

the objects that we have already quitted, .we shall have still greater reason to fear and stand in dread of the Divine punishment.

For he that recedes from the way of perfection, to return to what he has already quitted, shows that he is not content with God; and therefore, he deserves a greater punishment than he that never knew how sweet it is to live in poverty for the sake of God.

6. The more a man is exalted above worldlings when he quits all for the love of God, the lower he sinks beneath them, if after having tasted the sweetness of God, he depart from his good purpose.

The greater the honour and glory rendered to God by the vow of poverty, the more offensive is the injury offered to Him by one that neglects his vow for the sake of trifling objects.

And far better is it never to make a vow and to remain in the world, than to repent of thy vow, and be a source of scandal to thy brothers and the world.

CHAPTER II.

Of Religious Obedience.

1. IT should not be displeasing to thee to be ordered at times what is difficult and repugnant to the senses.

Nay, thou shouldst be glad and rejoice, that a most opportune occasion of profit is presented to thee.

If nothing difficult and unpleasant were ever enjoined thee, there would be no merit from the abnegation of thy own will in obedience.

Indeed one of the principal fruits of religious obedience would be lost.

It is very expedient that Superiors should sometimes command difficult things to mortify and purify the more, and that thou thyself mayest perceive how far thou art from perfection, seeing that thou has not thoroughly learned to yield to the will of Superiors.

Murmur not then against thy Superior, if perchance what he ordains please thee not, but require to be tried in every way, that so thou mayest better find out and correct thy imperfections.

2. Oftentimes that which is commanded, is not difficult; but still thou art troubled and dost rise up against it in thy interior.

The difficulty does not generally lie in the thing itself, but in the evil disposition of thy will.

Subdue thyself, and root out thy bad passions, and thou wilt find no cause for complaint in the order of thy Superior.

3. Whatever is commanded that is not sinful, should be fulfilled with joy; because the will of the Superior, is the will of God.

The more difficult the matter is, and the more repugnant to sensuality, the more eagerly should we obey and with greater joy of soul.

Because if easy things only are commanded, there might be reason to fear, that in the joy of the obedience, thou wert following thy own will without any merit.

But when thou art commanded what is difficult and displeasing to the flesh, thou art certain in obeying that thou performest the will of God, and with merit to thyself.

4. It is good for me, O Lord, to obey my Superiors for Thy sake, seeing that Thou Thyself, the Lord of the universe, didst for my sake become obedient to God and men, even unto the death of the cross.

Thou art the Saviour and Father of men, and orderest all things sweetly and mightily for our benefit.

How then can I hesitate or resist in obedience, since I am assured that submission to my Superiors places me under the merciful protection of Thy Providence?

Or what can I desire, but to serve Thee as Thou wilt, in humble obedience which cannot go astray.

5. I render thanks to Thee, O Lord, for having pointed out, and assigned to me so easy a path of salvation.

For, if for Thy sake I obey humbly and perfectly, I shall have nothing to fear in judgment.

Because though I may not have performed many great things in the sight of men, or have hidden and buried my talent for Thy sake, and not spread Thy glory further, behold, nothing will be laid to my account.

Obedience alone shall justify me, in which is contained all perfection, since it is the perfect fulfillment of Thy will.

Teach me, O Lord, to obey with humility and joy for Thy sake, and to prefer obedience to everything else.

For everything else is to be despised and reckoned for nothing, when there is question of executing what is known to be Thy will.

Chapter III.

Of Religious Chastity.

1. Nothing in the world is nobler and more worthy of admiration, than a voluntary and perpetual profession of chastity.

By it we are lifted above ourselves, and transported to things Divine, and though less than the Angels by nature, we become equal to them in dignity.

Yea, we are in a manner exalted above the Angels; for chastity is in them a condition of their nature, whereas in us it has the character of a great virtue.

They feel no wrestling of concupiscence; and in this respect they are the more perfect, whereas in us many conflicts arise in which we have great need of magnanimity and constancy not to be overcome; and in this we are more blessed than the Angels by reason of the merit.

The profession of chastity is a great help to us, in order, better and more freely to think the things that are of the Lord.

The heart is more easily torn from all

204 THE LOVE OF

creatures, when it has withdrawn itself from objects of pleasure, and cleaves to God in greater purity, and willingly seeks its rest in Him alone.

2. The profession of perpetual chastity is then a great treasure. But remember that *we have this treasure in earthen vessels.* It is a great virtue, but one that is exposed to many grievous trials, and requiring great watchfulness.

I see, saith the Apostle, *another law in my members fighting against the law of my mind and captivating me in the law of sin.*

And if the enemy of chastity lurks in the members of each one of us, we have indeed need of the greatest application not to be deceived and overthrown.

As the earth bringeth forth and nourisheth thorns, as wood is eaten away by worms; so doth this body of our mortality foster sensuality, by which the soul is often tainted and defiled; the soul, I mean, that is not most carefully guarded.

Nor can any one be secure, however much progress he may have made; for if thou desist but a little in thy watchfulness, behold the enemy falleth on thee unawares, and prepareth to slay thee, before even thou dost discover him.

3. Alas! how many terrible examples do we read of in the lives of the Saints, subjects of alarm to all, but especially to the negligent and lukewarm!

O depth of the incomprehensible judgments of God! *How is the gold become dim, the finest colour is changed?*

They that upreared themselves like columns and seemed to be firm, have fallen after many years of perfect life, and have in one moment cast away the splendour of the virtues, with which they were admirably adorned.

They that spread their wings like doves in the heavens, and built themselves a nest in the bosom of God, that they might not be tainted with the pollution of earthly stain, have fallen away, and miserably lain buried in the filth and abominations of this world.

They that were brought up in the scarlet of heavenly delights, and were filled with the manna of all sweetness, *have embraced the dung* of earthly things and filthy pleasures.

Truly, *the judgments of God are a great*

17

abyss; truly, *we ought to work out our sal-*
vation in fear and trembling.

4. Keep thou a strict guard over thyself,
lest what has happened to others that were
more perfect, more easily and quickly befall
thee.

It is the counsel of Heaven; *He that*
thinketh himself to stand, let him take heed lest
he fall.

Be afraid of the body betraying thee; for
it is a traitor.   It eats with thee, and drinks
and walks, and sleeps with thee; but it will
ever be thy bitterest enemy, when it sees
that it is loved too much and attended to
too carefully by thee.

Think how thou mayest rule over the
concupiscences of thy body; for the body
will either be thy slave or reduce thee to a
state of the harshest bondage, both here and
hereafter.

Watch over thy exterior senses, if thou
wilt preserve a clean heart, and avoid the
violent attacks of importunate imaginations.

Despise not a poor garment: let thy food
be sparing; for it is sufficient for health,
and be content with little sleep. *For he*
that nourisheth his servant delicately from his
childhood, afterwards shall find him stubborn.

Beware of too great familiarity with any one, and too much license of speech in conversation, however spiritual it may be at first; for the devil has caught many by this means.

Cut off all vain and superfluous cares; and believe not readily that thou hast need of many things, for the more thou shalt subtract from thyself, the more easily shalt thou maintain thy health of body and chastity.

Take away too at times and with discretion something of that which is necessary, and inflict some pain upon thy flesh, that thou mayest with the Apostle, chastise thy body and bring it into subjection.

5. It is very difficult for one that cares not to advance in other virtues, to preserve long his chastity; especially for one that struggles internally against obedience, curbs not his tongue, or confideth in himself, and takes a vain complacence in his own talents.

For God resists the proud, and in His mercy often allows that those whom He knows to have already sinned in secret from inward pride, should be humbled by some public sin of impurity.

It is impossible for one that does not pray, to remain chaste for a long time. For the nature of man is weak and frail, and prone to all sensuality; and God alone gives the holiness of so great a virtue; and He is wont to bestow this wonderful gift only on those, that by humble and earnest prayer make known to Him their desire to obtain it.

And as I knew, saith Solomon, that I could not otherwise be continent, except God gave it, and this also was a point of wisdom, to know whose gift it was, I went to the Lord, and besought Him with my whole heart.

If then thou wilt preserve this gem, this treasure, these wings for flying to God, this light for beholding heavenly things, chastity, let thy prayer to God be fervent, watch over thyself, shun private familiarities, humble thy soul.

No guard over ourselves will avail without the aid of prayer, no prayer without vigilance and mortification.

For both are necessary, according to the word of the Lord: *Watch and pray, that you enter not into temptation.*

CHAPTER IV.

Of the Abnegation of our own Will and Judgment

1. THE whole life of a good and true religious, is the constant abnegation of his own will and judgment.

If any one have undergone many long labours in doing his own will, it is nothing.

If he have written many beautiful and clever things, it is nothing.

If he have preached eloquently and gracefully, so as to fill his hearers with wonder and surprise, and to lead them from their evil path, in like manner it is nothing.

If he have gained for himself a great name for learning and skill in every science, this too is nothing.

If he have been placed in command over the rest, and shown great endowments of talent and prudence, and performed many things well, still it is nothing.

And if he work many great miracles, even so it is nothing: for many shall come to Christ on the day of judgment, saying, *Lord, Lord, have we not prophesied in Thy name, and cast out devils in Thy name?* But

17*

Christ shall profess unto them, saying: *Depart from Me; I know you not.*

2. But if he have done pennance for his sins and taken care to amend his vices, this is already something.

If he accept and undergo with patience, and even with joy, what he has to suffer in the observance of religious life, this also is something.

If he be diligent and fervent in prayer, recollected and humble in conversation, devoted and simple in obedience, this is already not a little.

But if he deliver himself up wholly to God, and inflamed with the desire of perfection, quit himself, and entirely renounce his own self-will, it is much, nay, it is a very great deal, it is everything.

3. This is that martyrdom, which, without demanding the shedding of blood, or presenting a dreadful picture of savage cruelty, is still more painful to the flesh by reason of its duration: for it must last until death.

This is that wonderful conflict, in which by the arms of justice on the right hand and on the left, we have to discomfit all the

onsets of the devil, until God receive us
into His Holy City of Sion, and crown us
with victory.

This is that straight path and that narrow
gate, of which Christ our Lord makes
mention, and by which all that have set
their hearts upon following in His footsteps, must advance and enter.

This is to take up one's cross daily, and
follow Jesus; nay, to put on Jesus, as the
Apostle commandeth.

4. Many imagine that they perfectly deny
their own will and judgment, but they are
grossly deceived.

For though they obey outwardly, still if
they look closely into themselves, scarcely
are they ever fully resigned in their interior.

Often the countenance is humble, and the
eyes are cast down, but the heart is full of
bitterness, obstinacy and obdurateness; and
we perceive it not, because we consider
ourselves too lightly.

Often some necessity, or politeness, or
solicitude to preserve our good fame, forces
us to dissemble the inward sentiments,
which the love of perfection should pluck

out from the very roots; and the malice of the will lies hidden in the heart.

Let us, I beseech you, open our eyes and look at ourselves attentively, and judge in sincerity. Is it not thus that hypocrites also act?

What doth it avail to seem good outwardly, and inwardly to be full of pride and blindness, and sensuality?

Men see those things that are without: *But God beholdeth the heart.* If then thou wilt please God, be solicitous about purity of heart, simplicity of good will, and internal virtues.

5. And if thou think thyself to have made great progress, see that thou errest not; a long way waits thee, and so much the longer, as perchance it seemeth to thee shorter.

He that knows but little, cannot know how much remains for him to learn.

But he again, that hath learned much, knows so much the better how much remains yet to be learned by him.

So they, that are still full of passions and unmortified in their will, often think that they have made sufficient progress; but holy and perfect men mourn, and think themselves very imperfect, for they see how much perfection they have still to acquire.

Therefore, give no credit to thyself; but rather deny thyself with all fervour, humble thyself, and spare not thyself, as often as thou hast failed to do so.

Thus must thou act, if thou wilt appear in the sight of God, a body without life, having the garments, but not the deeds of a religious, parading his name but showing no virtues, a wild fig tree, wasting all its sap in leaves alone.

Flatter not thyself; and think not thyself a good religious, unless thou hast learned to subdue thoroughly thine own will, and to bend it to the will of others.

CHAPTER V.

Of Useful Occupations.

1. SON, when I shall call thee, and thou shalt appear before My face to be judged, what wilt thou answer unto Me?

Many are the things of which I shall

demand an account; for many too are the obligations, which thou didst take upon thy shoulders, when thou didst enter into religion and accept My service.

And what excuse wilt thou plead, if thou hast squandered and reckoned at so poor a price the time that I have granted thee to labour in My vineyard?

Why dost thou not apply thyself with greater diligence to thine own sanctification, and the salvation of thy neighbour, and why dost thou throw away uselessly so many hours?

Take heed to thyself and to doctrine, be earnest in them.

2. Now thou wilt take heed to thyself, if, leaving all that does not conduce to thy progress, thou be urgent in good deeds, prayer and pious readings.

If thou often consider and examine thy life to see what must be cut off or mortified, or corrected or embraced.

If thou frequently take counsel with one of the more spiritual religious, chosen for his great virtue, to direct thee in spirit, and if thou obey him.

If thou execute with care what is ordered

by the Superiors, or prescribed in the rules of thy monastery.

If thou read and ponder the examples of the Saints, and be eager to imitate them.

If thou implore the Divine assistance before some pious picture, or in presence of the Most Holy Sacrament, to obtain constancy and success in thy good undertakings.

He, that with a true spirit of humility, and a sincere desire of advancing, performs these and other such things, takes heed to himself, and soon becomes a perfect man.

But now I will teach thee how to take heed to doctrine, that thou mayest assist thy neighbour with fruit to thyself.

But see that thou turn not imprudently against thyself the arms that are given to thee for thy neighbour's salvation.

For great peril is annexed thereunto, and it is far more necessary for thee to be on thy guard than it was for St. Paul, lest whilst thou preachest to others, thou thyself become a reprobate.

Now they turn these arms against themselves, who to take heed unto doctrine take not heed to themselves, and are not careful of their own amendment.

Such as these think not, that all the learning and wisdom of man can do nothing without the example of a life that is holy and altogether without reproof.

For, as the saying is, the voice of example is stronger than that of words.

For what men see done, they believe can be done; but what is preached only by voice and clamour, they resolve not so promptly to do.

4. What is it, My son, that leads men to Me, and makes them constant in good works?

It is not assuredly learning or great knowledge, or beautiful and sounding words, but My grace, and that spirit and life which is given to words by the union of the soul to Me, and the intimate knowledge and feeling of the eternal truths; and all this is obtained by prayer and compunction.

Thou hast heard what was said of old: this one hath planted, another hath watered; but God hath given the increase.

So it is; unless a man be intimately united to Me by prayer, and the abnegation of himself in all humility, vain is his knowledge and learning, and devoid of pleasure or relish.

5. Some even turn these arms against themselves, through their pride and haughtiness.

If they learn anything, speak anything, or do anything, they wish it to be known by all; yea, some learn, speak, and act solely through a desire of being honoured and accounted great men; and yet nothing can be more unbecoming than this in one, that is bound to seek perfection.

Fools and blind men! *They have received their reward*, because they preach themselves, and seek My glory in the last place.

They should profess with the Apostle that they know nothing, but Christ crucified; and on the contrary they are puffed up, and glory in profane and empty knowledge.

They should be most humble in their own eyes, who teach humility to others by their words, and make profession of it by their dress; and on the contrary they condemn and destroy in deed, what they insinuate by word and habit.

Upon them sentence has been already

18

past; *He, that hath,* yea, that preacheth to others, *My words, and despiseth them, hath one that shall judge him in the last day.*

6. Some love pursuits, that become not religious men, and lose their time to no purpose, and with great distraction and dissipation of mind.

What hast thou to do with things that feed curiosity, and belong to arts that delight much rather than assist?

What hast thou to do with politics, strange rumours, wars that are afar off, and opinions of wars?

All such things, unless they become worthy of commendation from the nature of one's life, or be enjoined for just reasons, are not to be embraced or even desired.

For they take away the soul very much from heavenly things, and often drive it upon the rocks of pride.

Meditate on the Scriptures, and thou shalt see how much thou wilt find that is useful for the conversion of thy neighbour.

Take counsel of theologians and holy writers: they will teach thee how thou shouldst seek, and happily succeed in obtaining the salvation of thy neighbour.

Peruse carefully the sacred histories and the lives of the Saints, and thou shalt learn what thou must do to become useful to the world.

7. For the world complains that religious have become useless, and idle, and ignorant,

And though its complaint is generally without foundation, still thou shouldst take care to become always more useful to the whole world, that thy entire order may not be reproached for thy idleness or vices.

Hear again what I have said before : *So let thy light shine before men, that they may see thy good works, and glorify thy Father, wdo is in Heaven.*

For it behooveth thee at times to appear before seculars, as one skilled in the science of the Saints, and in the Holy Scriptures, to let them know that they do not justly bring charges and accusations against religious.

Let them also know that nothing affords such pleasure to religious, as to be of service to all, with humility and sincerity, for the benefit of their souls.

Take heed then to thyself and to doctrine; be urgent in them, neither abound in idleness, nor become slothful.

For thus shalt thou save thyself, and those that hear thee. *But he that shall do and teach, he shall be called great in the Kingdom of Heaven.*

.

CHAPTER VI.

Of the Manner of Prayer in Dryness and Desolation of Soul.

1. SON, all consolation of spirit is a special gift of God, that is seldom, granted to the negligent, oftener, but not always, to the fervent.

Do not then despair, when thou art found dry and desolate in prayer or meditation; but rather humble thyself exceedingly, and say with the Prophet: *My heart is withered, because I forgot to eat my bread.*

And be not displeased, that thou canst not arrive at high contemplation; because the study of humility and patience is more necessary for thee.

At such a time then think over thy sins and defects, on account of which thou art deserted for a little while, and say with confidence, these and other such words:—

2. Lord, behold I know not how to pray; I blush to appear thus in Thy sight. Behold, *my soul is as earth without water unto Thee.*

Lord, I deserve in very deed this, and even still greater punishment for my sins and negligences.

Behold Thou hast left me to myself a little while, but not wholly deserted me, and I am become useless and lukewarm, that I may know how powerless I am without Thee.

It is good for me that Thou hast humbled me, that I may learn Thy justification.

Truly I am unworthy of Thy consolations, but do Thou cast Thine eyes upon me and have mercy on me, for I am weak, and infirm, and poor, and blind, and naked.

Show me, O Lord, Thy mercy, and grant me Thy salvation, that is my super-substantial bread and the joy of my soul.

For though it is not good to take the bread of the children and throw it to the dogs, still even the whelps eat of the crumbs that fall from their master's table.

18*

8. This humble prayer is most grateful to Me, and, if it be good for thee, I will give ear to thy supplication.

But meanwhile, resign thyself to My will, because I chide and chastise those whom I love; and persevere in thy good will, for the peace shall come that surpasseth all understanding.

Thou hast heard that it has been said: *The Lord, your God, trieth you, that it may appear whether you love Him or no.*

Therefore be courageous, be humble, be patient: *Let not your heart be troubled, and await the Lord.*

CHAPTER VII.

Of Inordinate Affection to Parents.

1. SON, I am thy father and thy mother: and having once become religious and left thy parents, thou shouldst not seek anything from them.

It pleaseth Me not, that thou sometimes revolvest in thy mind, that it is good and due to charity sometimes in the year to visit thy parents.

It is not love for thy parents, but rather thy own weakness and secret feebleness of mind, that requires this.

For thou seekest the consolation of man outside the monastery, because thy cell and compunction of heart grow not sweet to thee.

Thou seekest repose from the labour of observing thy institute, and the liberty which is according to human feeling.

Thou seekest delight and consolation from sensible things, because thou art void of spiritual joy, and lovest to live free from obedience and Superiors, that is, not according to the pleasure of My will.

2. Nor doth it avail that thy Superior yield to thy infirmity; for though a good and prudent Superior is not wont to consent easily, he gives way sometimes to avoid a greater evil.

This is not the spontaneous election of thy Superior, but thy own importunity and imperfection.

Thou thyself shouldst ask thy Superior not to allow thee to live out of the monastery without grave reasons, rather than foster thy carnal desires.

But alas! we have come to such a state, that he that asks and is refused, accuses his prudent Superior, and murmurs at the too great strictness of observance.

Thou shouldst render thanks to the Superior, when he fulfills the duties of his office with energy, and like a good physician, will not yield to thy infirmity.

3. What progress hast thou made, as often as thou hast gone to thy home? or what hast thou done for eternal life?

Behold I know what thou hast done; and therefore take heed to thyself and to compunction, for when the day shall come, I will judge thee.

Thou wilt find many more sins and defects in one month that thou didst spend with thy parents, than in one, or many years, under obedience in thy monastery.

Thou wilt find more faults to be purged in the fire from one short excursion to thy relations and friends, than thou hast acquired merits during a long time by compunction of soul, and austerity of life.

4. It is all'loss, if thou passeth from the monastery to thy relations even for a short time, although perchance they be good men or good women.

Because the love of liberty and vanity is not yet extinguished in thee; and the devil is far more powerful in the world against religious that are carnal and fond of roving.

In the paternal house, moreover, there are no exercises of spirit, such as are fitly provided in monasteries, and no Superior is on the watch there to admonish you, to deter and to correct.

5. Nor do I pour any sweetness into the souls of such religious, or promise them My wonted aid : *For it is not good to take the bread of children, and cast it to the dogs.*

Behold like dogs of the chase, breaking loose from their chains, they run up and down looking for some more delicate food; but they go very far astray, and are deceived.

For when they are outside the monastery, they entirely lose even the sweetness which is always present to him, that obeys for My sake; nor can they find any pleasure to compensate even slightly for the loss of this sweetness.

6. What thinkest thou are the thoughts of men, when they see a religious living and amusing himself freely with his parents?

Long since have I said: *No one is a prophet in his own country.*

Behold if thou hadst some name for sanctity, it is at once scattered all to the winds; nor do they think that he can be a spiritual man, that so easily leaves his monastery and his accustomed exercises of spirit; on the contrary, they are scandalized at the freeness of his manners.

7. But a still greater evil comes from it; for from thy fault a bad opinion of thy brethren is produced.

For men say not: *Such a monk did, or said this and that;* but they say: *Even monks say, or do this and that.*

Be then on thy guard, son, and take thee what thou dost; for My eye shall spare thee not, if in any way thou lessen the esteem due to thy brethren and My servants, by thy want of mortification and thy sensuality.

For he that touches their good fame, touches the apple of My eye.

8. But if charity really requires it, and thy Superior commands or freely permits thee to go home and stay with thy relations, hear what and how much is expedient.

Thy conversation with them should be holy and spiritual, and thy stay of the briefest, to give them to understand that thou art engaged in the things of God, and canst not comply with their desires.

Nor shouldst thou wander alone through the paternal house, or play, joke, and feast, for such things become not religious, neither hast thou learned them in the monastery.

But have a companion selected by thy Superior, and as soon as thou hast satisfied the claims of charity and duty, return with him in haste to the cloister.

9. Nevertheless, such times seldom come, and should not be sought for by thee.

The Saints often would not turn a little way out of their road to see their parents, although they might have done good to them by their example and conversation.

But thou, though imperfect and infirm, and scarcely knowing how to do good to thyself, dost seek for an excuse for going and staying with them ; and nevertheless, thou hast much greater reason to fear for thyself, than had those holy men of whom I have spoken.

It is not meet for one, that has abominated the desires of the flesh, for My sake, to follow them.

It is not safe for one, that should crucify his senses, to sit down to rich banquets.

It is not good for one that has vowed poverty, to sleep on soft couches.

It is not profitable to take amusement with seculars, after having renounced the world and its vanities.

It is not prudent for one that has resolved to serve God in chastity, to converse freely with women.

And therefore, whoever go too often to the house of their father or mother advance not in spirit, and in a short time lose the little they had gained before.

For *a man's enemies are they of his own household.*

Blessed is the man that renounces father and mother, and relations, for My name, provided he persevere; for such an one will be truly able to be My disciple, and son and brother.

And if any man hate not his father and mother, and brethren and sisters, for My sake, yea, and his own life also, he cannot be My disciple.

CHAPTER VIII.

Of Lowly Employments.

1. THE perfection of a religious does not consist in his doing things that appear great in the estimation of men, and being called a great or learned man.

But it consists in his doing the will of God, that is, in living perfectly in the place and position in which God, by means of his Superiors, has been pleased to direct.

This is the great truth which Jesus Christ ceased not to teach by His example during thirty years.

For He led a lowly life, and one that was almost useless and idle in the eyes of men.

He lay concealed from the world and despised, and looked down upon as a carpenter's son, even by those to whom He was known.

And yet He might have passed through towns and villages preaching, taught in the temple, and converted all sinners by the force of His miracles.

19

All this He might have done, and yet He did it not; that thou mightest learn to command and mortify thy excessive desire of being eminent in the world, and displaying thy talents.

2. O great mystery! that fills the humble with consolation, but the proud with confusion and reproach.

Behold Infinite Wisdom, the King of glory, the Lord of Heaven and earth, enriched pre-eminently with all the gifts of nature and grace, who had come into the world for the very purpose of waging war on vices, expelling errors, and rectifying morals; behold, I say, He lies hidden in a carpenter's workshop, and endures with the greatest patience the hardships of a poor life for thirty years.

But even whilst thus lying hidden, doing nothing for appearance, and burying His talents, He lived most perfectly, and made the greatest use of His talents.

The life of our Lord, which, in the eyes of men, appeared useless and abject; was, in the eyes of His Divine Father, most glorious and meritorious.

Because He lived as His Father willed,

did what His Father willed, was where His Father willed, and was silent when His Father willed.

Had Christ done great things before men all that time, He would have lived imperfectly, because He would not have fulfilled the will of His Divine Father.

3. Wherefore then dost thou think of making thyself known, when thou mayest in security lie hidden with Jesus in conformity to the Divine will?

Some speak not well that say: Why then has God given me a talent? is it not to increase it? and to hear at some future time: *Good and faithful servant, enter into the joy of thy Lord.*

They speak not well, I say, and are deceived, because they do not consider the merit of humble obedience.

Were it otherwise, why should God have bestowed the greatest talents upon Christ, our Lord, since He would not have Him use them publicly for thirty years?

4. Listen, thou proud and foolish man, God hath given thee these gifts of nature and grace, solely that thou mightest have something to sacrifice by obedience.

For the talents that are buried for the sake of God, lie not idle.

I call Heaven and earth to witness, said a certain one, that I had rather be a poor worm by the will of God, than a Seraphim on high, without it.

I had rather, with the will of God, do nothing, and be a martyr of idleness, than without it convert the whole world and be a martyr for the faith.

I had rather, with the will of God, lie hidden in some wretched corner under a bushel, than without it shine resplendent in the Heavens.

I had rather be a stock, with the will of God, than without it work miracles.

Provided always I execute what is well pleasing in Thy Divine sight, wherever I am, whatever I do, I am quite great enough, quite rich enough, quite happy enough, quite wise enough.

Chapter IX.

Of Curbing the Appetite.

1. He that knows not how to rule over his appetite, is easily vanquished by the devil, and led into the path of perdition.

For gluttony is the mother of idleness and dissipation, the fomenter of bad thoughts, the auxiliary of sensual motions, and the source of all carnal desires.

It takes away the strength of the soul by the fullness of the body, promotes scurrility, begets impatience, inconstancy, obstinacy, and arrogance.

O would to God, that we had not such frequent experience of this, even in religious communities!

How far greater would be our energy of soul, how far more fervent our zeal for the Divine glory, how far more becoming our conversation, and purer our conscience!

But because many yield and pay too much homage to their appetite, the observance of religious discipline waxes faint in them, and everything is full of murmurings, and idleness and vanity.

19*

For how shall one conquer the more spiritual deceits of luxury and the powers of darkness, that hath not learnt to resist this vilest of all enemies?

For though this vice is wont to inflict grievous injury, it is weaker and more easily overcome than the rest.

2. He that allows himself too much indulgence in food, is unfitted to pray well, and meditate fervently.

For the animal man doth not understand the things that are of God, and takes no pleasure in them, but wearies of and loathes whatsoever is not of the senses.

The soul of a carnal man, like a feather buried in the mud, cannot obey the breath of the Holy Spirit, cannot be torn from earth and fly towards Heaven.

Great abnegation of one's desires, is required for the soul to be in repose for meditation, and disposed for prayer.

And hence, when one is, as it were, poured out without measure over material food, he disdains spiritual banquets, and is not in a fit state to receive Divine consolations.

For why wouldst thou be visited and

consoled by God in a spiritual manner, if thou seek other consolations that are corporeal, inordinate, and contrary to the spirit of religion?

Take away the obstacles of vices; and thou shalt then be able to pray with fervour and devotion, and to taste heavenly things.

Make ready thy soul by abstinence and fasting, and then shalt thou hunger for the bread of life.

This has ever been the preparation made by the Saints for praying well;—to sleep little, fast much, afflict their flesh many ways: and sweet was their intercourse with God, and great their familiarity.

3. But if any one hold a different course, he will neither advance in the contemplative nor the active life: and will prove almost useless for very many good works.

A gross body is sluggish, weak, refractory, and demands more sleep and rest. Oftentimes it is ruined by superfluous nourishment, wasted in strength, and incapable of labouring well in the Lord's vineyard.

Thou wilt find no one that hath done much for the glory of God, and the salvation of souls, that has not first brought himself to temperance, yea, and even to abstinence.

Intemperance banishes God, scandalizes our neighbour, weakens the soul and body.

Doubtless, many beautiful things are thought of, but nothing is done; many good things are spoken, but the hearts of the audience are not pierced.

For their words lack the spirit of life, which God communicates not to the unmortified and sensual.

And if now and then thou see God make use of such imperfect men to bring about the conversion of sinners, deceive not thyself; but know that upon a time God prophesied even by the mouth of an ass. Now the one and the other should be accounted a great miracle.

4. On the other hand, temperance renders us useful to our neighbour, because it makes our mind see more clearly in human things, and be more intent upon the knowledge which is from God.

For it not only restrains the cravings of our appetite, but checks our pride, shakes off sloth, curbs the imagination, and raises the soul to the contemplation of God.

Temperance makes us hunger after heavenly food, opens the hidden things of the Scriptures, produces patience in labours, modesty, obedience and humility.

Temperance draws down the gifts of Heaven, and strikes to the ground the power of the tempter; and hence St. Peter saith: *Brethren, be sober and watch; because your adversary, the devil, as a roaring lion, goeth about seeking whom he may devour.*

Temperance, in fine, is most useful to the body itself, and frees it from many infirmities and pains.

Read the lives of the Saints; thou wilt find that the great Antony, and Paul, the hermit, and many others, lived to an extreme old age; and yet they not only merited commendation for their temperance, but even for most rigid abstinence and penance.

5. Be not then deceived; but see in what state thou art, and if thou be still the slave of thy appetite: let shame for thy folly stimulate thy efforts to begin now at least to deny thyself.

The body hath not need of much, nor of delicacies, or choice morsels; for many that are in great want, live on a poor and sparing diet, and still enjoy perfect health.

Think that thou also art a poor man, and the servant of a poor Lord: this thought will cheer thee up and be a motive for great temperance.

O that we endeavoured to imitate the example of Christ! truly, we should blush to become the menial servants of our body.

Let us often say to ourselves: *Christ hungered and thirsted for my sake; what then can be more unjust than for me not to be joyfully temperate for His sake.*

6. But some are so imperfect, as even by this pestilence of their sensuality to pollute and lead into a state of shameful grossness, the holy conversations of their brethren.

Our talk should not be of the delicacies of food: *For the Kingdom of Heaven is not meat and drink.*

All complaints about food are disgusting in the mouth of the religious; yea, and every suspicion of gluttony.

For where thy treasure is, there is thy heart also: and words proceed from the heart; for *from the abundance of the heart, the mouth speaketh.* Just then as it is a disgrace for a religious to set his heart upon so vile a thing, so also to converse about it.

Let our words be of God, and not of our food; of the delights of the spirit, and not those of the body; of eternal, and not temporal consolations.

Thus too will our words be calculated to give edification to all, and we ourselves shall advance in the love of God, and the knowledge of spiritual things.

CHAPTER X.

Of Spiritual Consolation.

1. So great is the excellence of spiritual gifts and the internal visitations of the soul by God, that even those that feel it, cannot sufficiently declare or comprehend its sweetness.

Never are we found so prompt and active as in time of such visitation.

Never do we offer ourselves with so great magnanimity and fortitude to God, to do with us as He will.

Never do we with such joy renounce ourselves, and even the least inordinate affections of our heart.

Everything is then considered most easy, nor is there anything which can deter us from taking the path to the highest sanctity.

2. Then indeed we understand how great is the happiness of the soul that offers itself wholly to God without reserve, and sets no bounds to its serving him in contempt, poverty and misery.

All this we then know full well, and view with as much rapture of soul, as if we were already saints, and freed from the weight of our body were already in possession of that wonderful bliss.

Then although our prayer be prolonged, no feeling of disgust is produced, nay, it is wont to be protracted for two or three hours with the greatest pleasure.

3. Neither do idle thoughts distract the soul, nor is the mind itself fatigued by this attentive inspection of itself, or wearied by the calm consideration of heavenly things.

For that, which then sustains, refreshes, and recreates it, descends from above and sweetly occupies it.

Then the wiles of the devil are clearly seen, good works are courageously proposed; nor do we say to God through·mere habit: *I am Thy servant.*

For we seem to be carried along by God in His holy service in a manner unknown to us before, and one that is not customary, but on the contrary, altogether singular, ineffable and celestial.

4. For the most part we do not know what great thing we have done for God, to merit such happiness.

For although God consoles whom He willeth, still He is wont to send these spiritual comforts in return for some good work or good disposition.

But if we examine our life closely, we shall see that these consolations and gifts from above are then especially given to us, when we have come to prayer with greater humility and purity of heart.

Now and then, too, it is because we have done something that went against nature and the flesh, and have been liberal towards God; and therefore, do we find God Himself, more liberal towards us.

5. For that promptness and alacrity,
20

which we feel at such a time in virtue, assuredly does not come from ourselves.

Nor do we at all understand how such marvellous sweetness, and such recollection and elevation of the soul can come from any one but God, who is *the God of all consolation.*

So great are they, that when we enjoy them, we think within ourselves, that it is good to become holy, even though this were the only happiness that fell to the lot of the Saints; and we say to Christ with Peter: *Lord, it is good for us to be here; let us make three tabernacles:*—one for the memory, one for the will, and one for the understanding.

O truly blessed self-denial, that draws down such blessings upon us!

O truly desirable compunction of soul, that is the source of so much good and so much pleasure to us!

O truly blessed practice of Divine meditation, by which God makes us so strong against evil affections, and adds such strength to our hope of sanctity.

6. If then thou wilt be frequently visited by God, be diligent in the service of God, in prayer, in penances; and be not like a man that tempts God.

For he tempts God, that expects sweet consolations from Him, and prepares not his soul for His visit, and is daily distracted without profit.

But if thou prepare a place for Him, and He come to thee flowing with delights, beware, lest thou begin to grow proud, and it be worse for thee.

For often, when God visits and fills us with joy, we propose to do great things, and we seem to ourselves to be freed and clear of all evil passions.

Those passions are not dead, but are taking a little rest, like dogs that desist from barking because they have food.

And think not thyself holy all at once, because thou dost foster holy desires; for it is one thing to desire, and another thing to execute what is holy.

CHAPTER XI.

Of Promoting Fraternal Charity in Ourselves.

1. *This is My commandment, that you love one another, as I have loved you.*

Love thy brothers for the sake of Christ, if thou wilt please Christ, thy first born brother.

Although thy brother be very imperfect and troublesome, still thou shouldst love him, that the precept of the Lord may be fulfilled: for thou too, though so great a sinner, wert the object of the most sincere love of our Lord.

O hapless state of certain religious! that think themselves spiritual men, and desire to labour in the ministries of apostolical charity amid distant and barbarous nations, and meantime care not for that domestic charity, which it is their bounden duty to observe.

Is not thy brother, that lives in the same monastery, partaker of the same food, and follows the same rule and discipline, nearer to thee than all the nations of barbarians?

Learn then first to exercise charity towards thy brethren, if thou wouldst, by charity, be useful to others.

Why seek a most difficult means of exercising charity amid remote peoples, thou that hast not yet learnt to suffer patiently the defects of thy brethren?

How wilt thou be prepared to shed thy blood, who canst not yet put up with a single word?

2. *By this shall all men know that you are My disciples, if you have love one for another.*

See the nobleness and excellence of charity! This is the virtue that makes and declares thee to be the disciple of Christ.

Since then nothing is more to be desired by man, than to be certified that he is a disciple of Christ, thou shouldst preserve and promote charity with solicitude.

And because nothing is more necessary for our neighbour, than to know and feel that we are from Christ, we are bound to give examples of charity.

Such is the force of evangelical charity, that by it every prejudice of worldly wisdom is easily overcome, even in the silence of the tongue.

For charity is something Divine, and both raises up men above themselves, and renders them most like unto God. For *God is charity.*

3. *Charity is patient, is kind; charity envieth not, dealeth not perversely; is not puffed up, is not ambitious, seeketh not her own.*

20 *

If thou canst not bear the defects of others, or console them in sorrow, and aid them in adversities, thou art void of charity.

If thou strivest to take for thyself what is better and more commodious; if thou wilt not cary the burden of another; if thou neglectest the care of not being disagreeable to others, thou hast not charity.

If thou judgest thyself to be better than another; if thou art wont to contemn the opinions of others; if thou converse not with modesty, sweetness and affability, thou art ignorant of charity.

Why wilt thou contend with thy brother about vain and trifling things, that concern thee not?

Hear the words of St. Paul: *The servant of the Lord must not wrangle; but be mild to all men, apt to teach, patient.*

Accordingly, it is a greater boon to maintain charity, than to gain with the loss of charity any victory whatsoever.

4. Virtue itself, cannot please God without charity, nor can it be called virtue.

Truly, patience is praiseworthy, humility is renowned, fortitude is glorious and temperance is excellent; *but if I have not charity, I am nothing.*

For charity, by which God is loved for His own sake, and our neighbour for the sake of God, is the greatest of all virtues, and the soul of all.

O how easily wouldst thou love thy brother, if thou didst love God! For one and the same is the motive for both loves— the supreme goodness of God; how then canst thou love God, and contemn thy brother?   •

How ready wouldst thou be for all offices of charity, if thou wert to think that thy brother is beloved by God, and is a member of the same body as thou art, under the same head, Christ our Lord!

Look at thyself; if one member suffer anything, do not all thy members suffer with it?

If thy foot be wounded, how solicitously dost thou seek for a remedy, how gently dost thou apply it, and how carefully dost thou handle the sore?

Do therefore in like manner to thy brother, though he be troublesome to thee; for thou shouldst love thy neighbour as thyself.

5. Wherefore, examine how thou mayest forestall all in kindness and attention; how

thou mayest with reason be disagreeable to none; how thou mayest exercise charity towards every one in word and deed without intermission.

Thou must endure the defects of all; satisfy all as far as may be done; if thou be not patient and agreeable, thou wilt not keep charity.

Abstain from singularities, and contemn privileges; love is stronger amongst equals; and therefore, the rule of common life should be kept by all, that would maintain the union of perfect charity.

If anything good befall thy brother, think it has fallen to thyself; be glad and congratulate him from thy heart. If any evil, think it has happened to thyself, be sorry and sympathise with him from thy very soul.

If he seeks anything, refuse him not; if anything annoys him, do it not; if he has formed a judgment or opinion about anything, resist it not.

Be gentle, meek, polite, humble of heart; do not contend, or murmur, ridicule not, satirize not, and unless it be thy duty, reprehend not.

6. *A triple cord is hardly broken; and a brother that is helped by his brother, is as a strong city.*

If charity shall bind us closely together, however much the devil may assault, or the world persecute us, we shall be happy.

But if charity begin to grow cold amongst us, though no one attacks from without, we shall not be in peace.

See then that thou offend not thy brother, or in any way whatever injure mutual charity, lest thou also wound thyself.

If thou offend any one, make him satisfaction as soon as possible; if any one offend thee, forgive him, and employ the same diligence for his cure, as if thou thyself had received the wound. For *we all offend in many things*, and none of us lives without fault: *If we say that we have no sin, we deceive ourselves, and the truth is not in us.*

And therefore, if at any time we think that we suffer something unjustly from others, let us accept it in punishment for our sins.

Let him that desires to be borne with, bear with others; let him that wishes to be loved, love others; let him that desires to be aided, aid others.

*If we love one another, God abideth in us,
and His charity is perfected in us.*

CHAPTER XII.

Of the Choice and Perfection of Virtues.

1. So long as we are weighed down by our mortal flesh, we cannot acquire the perfection of all virtues ; and therefore, we have need of selection that we may not labour in vain.

Choose then a virtue to practise, until, by the assistance of God, thou become most perfect in it.

Some virtues are continually called for in our daily actions, and are necessary for all ; and therefore, should be acquired with particular industry.

The more thou shalt make progress in meekness, patience, modesty, temperance, humility, and others, that come into more frequent use, the sooner wilt thou become holy.

2. Some seek after virtues which have a

greater appearance of nobility, and are reckoned amongst men to be more glorious.

They instruct with pleasure, but it must be in famous churches, and to a large assembly of noble and learned men.

They visit the sick with pleasure, and hear confessions, but only of those that are conspicuous for riches or honours.

See that thou set not a high value upon these things: it is more perfect and safer to imitate Christ our Lord, and to go about villages, than to hunt for the praise of eloquence and learning in cities.

It is more useful to thee to visit and console the poor and the rude, than the rich and noble, who, moreover, are less prepared to listen to and obey thy words.

3. Some are content with the virtues that agree with their natural inclinations; because they seem easier, and require not any, or a less violent struggle.

But when they have need of self-denial and mortification, they have not the courage to practise virtue; but they lose heart, turn faint-hearted, and think it is best to spare themselves.

Do thou follow them not, for they that

are such, make no progress, but rather fall away from the way of perfection, because they follow not the teaching and example of Christ.

For it was not those who spare themselves, and fear the hardship of the struggle, whom Christ declared blessed, but those that mourn, and fight manfully for justice sake.

Christ Himself would be a man of sorrows, and be saturated with reproaches, and accounted a worm and no man.

Christ also saith : *I came not to send peace, but the sword.* And, *if any man will come after Me, let him deny himself, take up his cross and follow Me.*

4. Choose then what is most contrary to nature, and thou shalt make rapid and secure progress.

Choose the study of patience, humiliation, and every kind of self-denial; this is the way of perfection, this is the foundation of the spiritual life.

If thou learn to overcome thyself, thou wilt quickly acquire other virtues, magnanimity, fortitude, obedience, fraternal charity, in fine, freedom from all inordinate affections.

But if thou give no thought to denial of thyself, in troubles and adversities thou wilt be impatient, sad, cowardly, useless to thyself, and a subject of scandal to others.

Wherever thou art, whatever be thy occupation, some occasion for fighting is always at hand, nor can it always be shunned: unless then thou learn to fight, thou wilt quickly fall beneath its assaults.

5. Many labour to acquire virtues, but are not particular about the perfection of those virtues, and hence they remain for ever weak and infirm.

We must not rest satisfied with mediocrity; we must never say, *it is enough;* but labour to ascend to the very highest perfection.

It is a sign of a mean and paltry spirit, to stand still in the pursuit of virtues, and to turn with disgust from greater sanctity.

Let us seek to approach to virtues such as they were in Christ, that each one may say: *Be you imitators of me, as I also am of Christ.*

6. Let our humility be such, and let it bring us down so low, that we turn not away from any debasement and confusion.

21

Let our obedience be such as to remain constant unto death, saying: *Not my will, but Thine be done.*

Let such be our charity to our neighbours, even those that are inimical and hostile to us, that each one shall desire to be anathema from Christ for his brethren, and to lay down his life for their salvation.

For all these things hath Christ done for us, *leaving us an example, that we follow in His footsteps.*

But if thou restest satisfied with mediocrity in virtue, O beware! for thou shalt fall short of even that mediocrity, and when danger shall come upon thee, thou shalt find thyself on the point of perishing.

THE END.

Standard School Books.

Fredet's Ancient and Modern Histories.

New Revised and Enlarged Editions, Continued up to 1867.

Ancient History ; fr‹ n the dispersion of the Sons of Noe, to the Battle of Actium, and the change of the Roman Republic into an Empire. By PETER FREDET, D. D., Professor of History in St. Mary's College, Baltimore. 20th edition, carefully revised and enlarged..............12o. half arabesque, 1 50

Modern History ; from the coming of Christ, and the change of the Roman Republic into an Empire, to the Year of our Lord, 1867. By PETER FREDET, D. D., Professor of History in St. Mary's College, Baltimore. 24th revised, enlarged and improved edition.....................12o. half arabesque, 1 50

Introduced into many of the principal Literary Institutions of the United States, adopted as Text Books in the Irish University, Dublin, and many Institutions in England and the Provinces, Fredet's Histories have acquired a wide-spred reputation, and their excellence is too well established, at this day, to be dwelt upon. The publishers have the pleasure of announcing that in order to make the Modern History more complete and deserving of the liberal patronage hitherto extended to it, they have, with the valuable assistance of the late Dr. Fredet's reverend collaborators, added several Chapters embracing the Historical Events that have taken place in this and other countries from 1854 to 1867.

The Modern History has been thoroughly revised and considerably enlarged. The additional matter, carefully prepared, will be found worthy of the distinguished Historian's original work. The history of the Recent Civil War in the United States, particularly, has been compiled with a truthful impartiality, which makes it the best Synopsis of this Memorable Event yet published for the use of Educational Institutions. It is a correct record of facts, faithfully told without political comment.

The student will therefore find in Dr. Fredet's two books, the "Ancient" and "Modern" Histories, the most Complete, Authentic, and reliable *History* of the *World*, from its Creation to the Year of our Lord, 1867.

MURPHY & Co. *Publishers & Booksellers, Baltimore.*

Standard School Books.

Fredet's Ancient & Modern Histories.

☞ *From a large number of Commendatory Notices, we select the following, as embodying the spirit of all.*

COLLEGE OF WILLIAM AND MARY, *Williamsburg, Va.*

MESSRS. J. MURPHY & CO.,   *October*, 1867.

GENTLEMEN:—The demand for Fredet's Ancient and Modern Histories and Kerney's Compendium of History, shows that these most excellent books are appreciated as they ought to be. The improvements and additions to the editions of 1867 just issued from your press, make them all that could be reasonably desired. Immediately after the reopening of the College of William and Mary in 1865, Fredet's Histories were, after a careful examination of the Text Books of the day, adopted in the Institution. A more intimate acquaintance soon justified the wisdom of the selection. They evidently were written in a conscientious and Christian spirit, with a manifest intent to teach historical truths. They constitute an honorable monument to the memory of the late Reverend Author.

Kerney's Compendium was subsequently introduced into the College Grammar School, and gave entire satisfaction. In style and system and the interest it excites, it is admirably adapted to beginners and junior students, while it may be read and consulted with profit by the more advanced. Trusting that your public spirit and enterprise in putting such standard works within reach may meet with a liberal encouragement, I remain

Yours, Very Respectfully,   BENJ. S. EWELL, *President,*
                                                College William and Mary.

The *Metropolitan* says:—"The style is veritably charming by its simplicity, and by the quiet love of his subject which the reverend author displays. It is the language of a talented and successful teacher, who relates to his class the great events of time, succinctly but graphically, without bombast, yet in a lively and picturesque manner. It is thus that history should be written for youth."

The *London Standard* says: "These two excellent manuals of History have a wide and increasing circulation in America, and are everywhere held in the highest esteem. The compiler, Dr. Fredet, has achieved a task of no ordinary difficulty, in compressing so much recondite matter into so small a space; in leaving untold nothing that was of note of the immense and varied annals of the world. No college, school, or library ought to be without these excellent works."

The *Dublin Telegraph* says: "Fredet's Histories have been adopted, as a class-book, by the Irish University; and we entertain no doubt, that they will soon supersede, even in other establishments, those miserable compilations which wilful perverters of truth have long palmed upon the public as histories and abridgments of histories."

MURPHY & CO. *Publishers & Booksellers, Baltimore.*

2

Kerney's Compendium

Of Ancient and Modern History.

New Revised and Enlarged Edition, Continued up to 1867.

A Compendium of Ancient and Modern History, from the Creation to the year 1867, with QUESTIONS, adapted to the use of Schools and Academies; also an APPENDIX, containing the Declaration of Independence, the Constitution of the United States, a Biographical Sketch of Eminent Personages, with a Chronological Table of Remarkable Events, Discoveries, Improvements, etc. By M. J. KERNEY, A. M. 32d revised edition.........................12o. half arabesque, 1 25

In presenting a Revised and Enlarged Edition of this Popular History to the public, the publishers deem it unnecessary to dwell upon its merits. Extensively introduced into the Schools of this Country and in many Institutions of Learning in England and Ireland, and even in the East Indies, it has met everywhere with the greatest favor, and twenty-nine editions rapidly exhausted are evidence of the liberal patronage extended to this sterling work.

The Compendium has been brought down to the Present Time, and this Edition comprises all the Important Events that have transpired in Europe since the Crimean War, including the Recent War between Austria and Prussia; the History of the Ephemeral Empire of Mexico; and a Graphic Sketch of the American Civil War, *written without partiality or bias.* The data for this Last and Important Chapter have been carefully compiled from the most authentic sources, and form the *best Narrative of the Principal Events of the War, that can be put into the hands of the young.*

·These additions have been carefully prepared, and written in conformity with the spirit of impartiality which has made Mr. Kerney's books so popular.

RECOMMENDATIONS.

Kerney's Compendium has been introduced into the College Grammar School, and gives entire satisfaction. In style and system, and the interest it excites, it is admirably adapted to beginners and junior students, while it may be read and consulted with profit by the more advanced.   BENJ. S. EWELL, *President,*

College William and Mary.

WILLIAMSBURG, VA., *October,* 1867.

MURPHY & Co. *Publishers & Booksellers, Baltimore.*

8

Kerney's Compendium of History.

Standard School Books.

School Edition of Lingard's England.

Abridgment of the History of England. By JOHN LINGARD, D. D. With a Continuation from 1688 to the Reign of Queen Victoria. By JAMES BURKE, Esq. To which are added, Marginal Notes and Questions, adapted to the use of Schools, by M. J. Kerney, A. M. 9th ed. 700 pages, 12o. half arab., ... 1 50

The student will find that the ipsissima verba of the great Historian of England has been religiously preserved in the Abridgment.

Of the Continuation we shall merely say, that it has been written by an author who has been long and favorably known in literature.

NOTICES OF THE PRESS.

The Metropolitan, in noticing this work, says:—"We are glad to see this excellent abridgment adapted to the use of schools. It will do much to remove those many false impressions, which English historians have hitherto made upon the readers of history by their word-painting of imaginary events. In no nation perhaps was history more 'a conspiracy against truth,' than in that of England, and in none did the mind of American youth need a more particular antidote to its poisoning influence. It was a good thought then to give a sound, reliable first-book to the youthful student, and we are happy to find that Mr. Burke and his able American collaborator, have succeeded in producing a text-book which we can with the utmost confidence commend to the favorable consideration of the instructors of youth."

The *Cambridge* (Mass.) *Chronicle* says:—"We have often called the attention of our readers to the great value of Lingard's History. The learning, ability, and general impartiality of the author are well known. An abridgment of the work was very desirable, and it appears to have been very well done by the present editor. No person can be said to be thoroughly acquainted with English History who is not familiar with Lingard. The volume is well printed, in a clear type and convenient form, and furnishes a valuable contribution to the historical literature of the country."

The *London Critic* says:—"The author has carefully and successfully produced a volume that must be very acceptable to those for whose use it was designed."

MURPHY & Co. *Publishers & Booksellers, Baltimore.*

5

Standard School Books.

Upwards of 50,000 Copies, of the Old Edition, have been sold.

The First Class Book of History, designed for pupils commencing the Study of History; with QUESTIONS, adapted to the use of Academies and Schools. By M. J. KERNEY, A. M. 23d Revised and Enlarged Edition...... 60

From the Preface to the Twenty-Second Enlarged and Revised Edition. — Eighteen years of uninterrupted success have established the superior excellence of Kerney's First Class Book of History. Teachers having frequently expressed regret that the author had confined himself to Modern Times, instead of embracing in his plan the outlines of Ancient History, as he has done so successfully in his larger work, the "Compendium of Ancient and Modern History," the Publishers have sought, in the present edition, to bring this valuable little book to a state of completion which would leave nothing to desire. They have confided this task to a gentleman of experience, who has added to Mr. Kerney's work a short but complete Synopsis of Sacred and Ancient History, together with an interesting chapter on the Progress of Civilization. The Book might now be aptly styled "The First Class Book in Universal History."

In addition to this entirely new matter, the Modern History has been enlarged by the introduction of several chapters, embracing the most important and recent events that have transpired in the civilized countries of the world, including the late American Civil War.

No pains have been spared in the revision and preparation of this Edition, with the hope of rendering it worthy, in every respect, of the high commendation and liberal patronage enjoyed by Mr. Kerney's Popular Class Books.

EXTRACTS FROM NOTICES, &c.

Messrs. J. MURPHY & Co.   BALTIMORE, *May* 28, 1868.

Gentlemen: — I have carefully examined your new edition of the First Class Book of History, and I beg to express to you the satisfaction I have felt in its perusal. It is admirably adapted to the purposes of a text-book; the arrangement being such that it is calculated to fix in the youthful mind impressions rendered vivid by the easy, natural and interesting style of the narrative.

As a practical evidence of my appreciation of the merits of this book, permit me to assure you of my determination to adopt it in my own school.   Very respectfully,   HENRY ONDERDONK.

MURPHY & Co. *Publishers & Booksellers, Baltimore.*

7

First Class Book of History.

A Catechism of Scripture History, compiled by the Sisters of Mercy for the use of the children attending their schools. Revised and corrected by M. J. Kenney, A. M. 20th Edition. 18mo. half cloth......   75

"This excellent work is now used in nearly all Catholic institutions throughout England and Ireland, and has also acquired an extensive circulation throughout the neighboring republic.

"The object of the Catechism, according to the preface, 'is to render children early acquainted with the truthful and interesting events recorded in the sacred Scriptures; to familiarize them with the prophecies relating to the coming of the Messiah, and lead them to regard the Old Testament as a figure and a foreshadowing of the New.'

"The present edition has been much improved, the questions to the answers being made more concise, so as to admit of their being easily committed to memory. An appendix has also been added, containing extracts from the Prophets, Scripture texts, and short sketches of the lives of the Apostles and Evangelists. The Chronological Table, which has been carefully revised and considerably enlarged, fixes the dates of the most remarkable events recorded in the Sacred Writings.

"We hope soon to see the work introduced into all Catholic Schools in the British Provinces, and were its merits fully known, we are pretty certain it would meet with a circulation similar to that which it has acquired in England and the United States."

Halifax Catholic.

"Of the merits of the book itself, it would be superfluous to speak, but we may observe that the labors of the American editor have added very considerably to its value."   *Metropolitan.*

"It is an admirable book for schools, and calculated to give a far more vivid and lasting knowledge of sacred history than could be obtained from years of desultory and mechanical 'Bible-reading.'"

Detroit Vindicator.

Catechism of Ecclesiastical History. Abridged for the use of Schools. Translated from the French by a Friend of Youth. A New Enlarged Edition................... ....16o. flex. cloth,   80

This little work has been carefully revised and enlarged, the text being brought down to the present time. These improvements it is hoped will render it still more popular with the instructors of youth.

Murphy & Co. *Publishers & Booksellers, Baltimore.*

Standard School Books.

Kerney's Murray's Grammar.—*An Abridgment of Murray's Grammar and Exercises*, designed for the use of Academies and Schools; with an Appendix, containing Rules for Writing with Perspicuity and Accuracy; also a Treatise on Epistolary Composition. By M. J. KERNEY, A. M. 37th edition,.................18o. hf. bd. 25

This Grammar is used in the Public Schools of Baltimore; in the Schools of the Christian Brothers; and in many of the principal Schools and Academies throughout the country.

In point of arrangement, this work is superior to any other Abridgment of Murray's Grammar that has yet appeared before the public. It combines the Grammar and Exercise, by adapting Exercises to every chapter and section throughout the work, so that the pupil may have, at every stage of his progress, a practical illustration of the portion under his immediate study. The present edition has been carefully revised by the author, and many valuable improvements made in the work. A Treatise on Epistolary Composition has been added, containing directions for writing Letters, Notes, Cards, &c., with a variety of examples of the same.

EXTRACTS FROM NOTICES OF THE PRESS.

"This abbreviation of the large and unwieldy volume of the Patriarch of Grammarians has been effected without the omission of any important matter, and is presented to the public in a neat and convenient form. It must find favor in schools."—*Balt. Pat.*

"We most cheerfully recommend this *Grammar* to Schools."
St. Louis News-Letter.

"This is an excellent abridgment of Murray, long a favorite in schools." *Fred. Examiner.*

Murray's Grammar.

Murray's English Grammar, adapted to the different classes of learners; with an APPENDIX, containing rules and observations for assisting the more advanced students to write with perspicuity and accuracy. By LINDLEY MURRAY. 12o. half bound, 40

In presenting a new edition of Murray's Grammar, which is universally considered the best extant, we deem it sufficient to state, that the present edition is printed from an entirely new set of plates, and that it has been carefully revised, and free from many of the inaccuracies and blemishes which are to be found in other editions, printed from old stereotype plates. This, together with the very low price affixed to it, are the only claims urged in favor of this edition.

Murray's English Reader...........18o. 35

MURPHY & Co., *Publishers & Booksellers, Baltimore.*
14

Wettenhall's Greek Grammar.—*Rudiments of the Greek Language*, arranged for the Students of Loyola College, Baltimore, — upon the basis of WETTENHALL. 6th. ed. 12o. half arabesque,   75

Extract from the Preface.— "It is not intended by this publication to present a new Greek Grammar to the classical student; after the elaborate volumes of Matthiæ, Buttman, Kuhner, Gail, Burnouf, and other scholars of Germany and France; it would be altogether vain to expect any new discovery in that language. The most that we can do is to avail ourselves of their labors in order to smooth the difficulties, which are usually met in its study. The greatest of these, we have learned from a long experience in teaching, is the large size of the grammars, which are put in the student's hands when he commences. Excellent as these may be for the professor or more advanced scholar, they only tend to deter the beginner from approaching it. We trust that this will be obviated by the present compendium, in which we have endeavored to comprise within as short a compass as possible, all that is of absolute necessity to the learner. If it induces him to apply with more alacrity to study a language second to none in the literary beauties and treasures which it contains, our intentions will have been amply fulfilled."

"We commend it most heartily to those who wish to study that most perfect of all human languages, as the shortest and readiest way to smooth all their difficulties."   *Metropolitan.*

Ruddiman's Latin Grammar. — *Ruddiman's Rudiments of the Latin Tongue;* or, a Plain and Easy Introduction to Latin Grammar: wherein the principles of the language are methodically digested, both in the English and Latin. With useful Notes and Observations. 30th edition — corrected and improved. By WILLIAM MANN, M. A. 12o, half arabesque...........................   75

☞ *The cheapest and best Latin Grammar published.*

Ars Rhetorica—Auctore, R. P., MARTINO DU CYGNE, Societatis Jesu. Editio Secunda Americana. In usum Collegii Georgeopolitani, S. J. 18o. half arab.................................   75

To this New Edition, an Appendix has been added, containing Examples taken from the English Classics.

MURPHY & Co. *Publishers & Booksellers, Baltimore.*

The North American Spelling Book.

Designed for Elementary Introduction in Schools. A New Enlarged Edition, being an improvement upon all others. 18 cents.........per dozen, 1 62

The aim in this compilation has been to present a gradation of lessons necessary to impart a knowledge of the spelling, division, pronunciation, and accentuation of the various sounds and syllables that compose the English language. In pronouncing and accenting words, good usage and the best lexicographers have been followed. The rules laid down are few, but simple and concise; and the progress from what is easy to what is difficult, is gentle and gradual. It is universally conceded to be one of the BEST, as it is unquestionably the *cheapest Spelling Book published.*

German School Books.

☞ The following Books, prepared by the Superiors of the Society of the Holy Redeemer, in Baltimore, are extensively used in German Schools throughout the United States.

A B C und Buchstabir und Lesebuch,   15
Katholischer Katechismus..........18o.   30
Biblische Geschichte des Alten und
   Neuen Testaments......................   40
Kleiner Katechismus, 3 cts. ; per 100,   2 00

☞ The following GERMAN SPELLER and READER have been carefully prepared by the School Sisters of Notre Dame, expressly for the German Schools under their charge. They may justly be considered the best Books of their class for the use of German Primary Schools.

Fibel für die lieben Kleinen, gebraucht in
   den Schulen der deutschen Schulschwestern
   unserer Lieben Frau............................   10

Lesebüchlein für die lieben Kleinen, gebraucht in den Schulen der deutschen Schulschwestern unserer Lieben Frau...............   15

Gillespie's Progressive System,
PENMANSHIP,

In 6 Numbers, with Steel Plate Copies at the Head of each Page.

Price, per Number, 18 cents..........per Dozen, 1.50.

This system is designed to lead the pupil from the first principles in Penmanship to a free, open, practical style of writing, adapted to general business purposes.

Having purchased the Plates and Copyright of this Series of COPY BOOKS, we respectfully solicit for them a careful examination, which is all that is necessary to prove the superiority, utility, and economy of this system.

MURPHY & Co. *Publishers & Booksellers, Baltimore.*